Dead Nasty

Helen H. Durrant

DEAD NASTY

Detectives Calladine & Bayliss Book 6

JOFFE BOOKS

Revised edition 2025
Joffe Books, London
www.joffebooks.com

First published in Great Britain in 2016

This paperback edition was fist published
in Great Britain in 2025

Cover art by Nick Castle

ISBN: 978-1-80573-032-3

PROLOGUE

Elsa Ramsden woke up with a start. She felt weird. Bad dream? Too much booze? No, not this time. This was something different.

She was in a strange room, dark and foul smelling. Panic churned in her belly. Every instinct told her to get out — fast. But she couldn't move. One fearful look down told her why. Thick, black tape bound her to a chair. But the nightmare didn't end there. A man wearing a hood with holes cut out for his eyes, was standing in front of her, staring. This had to be someone's idea of joke. Except that it wasn't funny.

"Who the fuck are you? What the hell am I doing here?" she spat at him.

He said nothing.

"Speak to me, freak!" she screamed at the hooded face, trying to wrench her hands free.

What had happened? The events of the past few days flashed through her head. And then she got it. "This is down to Gaby, isn't it?" Anger at being tricked was an effective antidote to the fear. "She's told her dad what we did. She's got that murdering father of hers to set this up. I'm right, aren't I?"

"If I were you, Elsa, I'd shut up and save my strength."

1

He knew her name. The voice was disguised, but the accent was local. "I'll bloody kill her! The bitch has gone too far. Trust Gaby Donnelly to pull a sick stunt like this. And all because of a stupid photo!"

He knelt down and put his hooded face close to hers. "This is all about you and me, Elsa. It has nothing to do with anyone else."

He looked into her eyes. A few seconds of silence followed. Elsa couldn't see anything but the hood and two dark eyes, but she knew he was grinning at her.

She hissed, "There is no *you and me*, creep! Why am I really here?"

He ran a finger down her cheek — a gesture of affection that made her cringe. He spoke softly, almost lovingly. "You're here to die, Elsa."

He meant it. This man was a nutter, and there was nothing Elsa could do. The realisation sliced through her guts like a dagger. Bile rose in her throat and she choked. Her head spun. Her headache and confusion told Elsa that she'd been drugged. This, and the fear, clouded her judgement. She couldn't think straight.

"You're kidding me! You have to be. You need to let me go." The words tumbled out, though she knew it was no joke. "Tell Gaby or whoever, that it worked. I'm . . . scared. Alright? Scared out of my skull, and sorry. Job done." Elsa's voice faltered. She began to shake.

No reply. He moved into the shadows at the far end of the room. She couldn't see him properly, but she did see the flare of a match. The apology had cut no ice. Time to fight back. She screamed, "Did you hear me, freak? Why don't you fucking listen?"

"Language, Elsa."

"This is down to Gaby, I know it. But she got everything that was coming to her. Stupid slag! It isn't all one-sided, you know. She's a vindictive cow."

"Calm down."

"Piss off!" she barked back, trying to wriggle free. "And tell Gaby to stuff it! I'm not frightened of her! Or you! You have to let me go." Suddenly Elsa sneezed. Her chest was tightening. "I have asthma. There's something in here I'm allergic to. I have to get out before I get worse."

"In that case I'll make this quick." He was close again, leaning over her. And he had a hypodermic in his hand. "You don't look well, Elsa. Your eyes are puffy and you're wheezing."

"I told you, I'm allergic to stuff. You, for a start!" She pulled against the tape again.

"You won't have to worry for much longer. I'm going to put you out of your misery." The laugh that followed these words cut right through her.

"You have to release me. Don't you know who I am?"

He laughed again. "You're just some stupid schoolgirl. No one likes you — you upset people. No one will care when you're gone."

Defiant, she pulled against the tape. "My family are right hard nuts. You must have heard of the Ramsdens. My brothers will do you proper if you don't let me go."

More laughter.

Somehow, Elsa had been stupid enough to walk right into this one. She yanked on the bindings again. "How did I get here? I was going to Megan's." She couldn't work it out, her memory was hazy. She remembered being on her friend's street and texting her to hurry up. What had happened after that?

He raised the syringe and she leaned away. "What's in that thing?"

"Morphine."

"Bugger off! Don't put that thing anywhere near me."

"You're going to need it."

There was a sharp scratch in her arm and her stomach clenched again in terror.

"Let the drug do its work." He patted her hand. "Now, it's time to put a few things right. No more cruel texts," he

3

ran his fingers gently over her cheeks and lips, "And no more harsh words."

The feel of his fingers moving over her face made her feel sick.

"It will be better if you're out of it for what comes next."

What did that mean? She tried to talk, but the words wouldn't come. "Let . . . let me go . . ." Her head lolled forward. Why couldn't she speak? And what was that smell? Petrol, or something. She looked down. He'd wrapped a roll of cloth around her right hand and wrist and fastened it tight with tape. In her confused state it seemed as if things floated towards her, out of thin air. A bottle. He was pouring fluid onto the cloth.

One of her arms was free. He'd cut the tape binding her right wrist to the chair. This was Elsa's chance, but only if she sharpened up. She took a deep breath, hoping to clear her head. Hit out, make the blow count. But she was too slow. His hand gripped her upper arm. The smell of petrol grew stronger, the fumes making her eyes water.

There was a sudden flare, as he lit another match. Then the penny dropped. Vomit rose in her throat. There was nothing she could do. As the cloth wrapped around her hand burst into flame, Elsa threw up. She heard him count — one . . . two . . . three.

But Elsa was unconscious before he finished.

CHAPTER 1

Tuesday

"You've made a big dent in your blood pressure, Tom."

"I took all the advice everyone threw at me, doc. Been going to the gym and cut down on the booze." Tom Calladine clapped his belly. "Lost nearly a stone and a half."

Doc Hoyle's face lit up in a smile. "Glad to hear it. For a while you had me worried, you were going downhill fast. But you've cracked it. I was half expecting you to just tickle around the edges of the healthy-living thing. But you've done great. You're looking good, too. That's a new suit you've got there." He leaned forward and rubbed the cloth of Calladine's jacket which was lying across the chair.

The detective smiled. "My old clothes don't fit anymore, what with the diet and the gym. I have to admit, I do feel better."

"Hair's an improvement."

"I've had it cut short again. Doesn't show so much grey."

"Everything you've done makes my job a whole lot easier. I don't have to make up a fairy tale. The force would have you out on your arse if your fitness deteriorated below a certain

5

level. What you have to do now is keep it up. At your age, Tom, too much beer and junk food will take years off your life. Bob Bradshaw had a heart attack last week. He's not a patient here, so I can tell you that."

"I went to school with him!" Calladine exclaimed. "We were in the same year."

"I know you were. It knocked me back with a wallop too. He's another one who fell into the trap of putting his work first. He was always on the road in that truck of his. Took all his meals at motorway cafes. He'll probably have to retire now."

"Won't suit him. He's a worker, like us. What's happened to you anyway? You're doing more than ever here. Retirement not up to scratch?"

"I get bored. Two days a week, that's quite enough retirement. Otherwise I go mad. I have the shed, go for walks with the wife, and we lunch out. It keeps me fresh. You not ready to give it a go yet? Do you good, you know."

Calladine shook his head emphatically. "No way. Work suits me just fine."

"Don't forget holidays. It's always good to have a break."

"Actually, doc, we have been making plans."

"You and that new woman of yours? I can't say I blame you. But be careful. She's not got the miles on the clock. She's at least ten years younger than you."

The doc was right of course. But Calladine didn't want it shoving down his throat. He couldn't help it if younger women were attracted to him. "What're you writing?"

"Your medical report, and it's all good. You've worked hard and you're in tiptop condition. All you have to do now is keep up the good work."

"I'll do my best.

"My advice, if you'll take it: don't eat on the hoof. And none of those canteen breakfasts. Try to keep the booze to a minimum, and you should be fine."

"I've got this far, there'll be no slacking now. But it's been hard. All that salad stuff played havoc with my guts

6

at first. The gym's great but it takes up time. But the worst was the Wheatsheaf, and the obligatory pint or two at the end of the day. But now I limit it to one, and then toddle off home."

Calladine's father had died far too young from heart problems. He was well aware that he needed to follow the doctor's advice, and get things under control.

The doc shook his head. "I see it all the time. Blokes reach your age and still behave as if they were in their teens. You can get dressed now. I'll send the report in by the end of the week. There should be no problems."

"Thanks, doc. But you don't look so hot yourself."

"Backache — gardening all weekend. Overdid it."

Calladine smiled as he did up his shirt. "Perhaps I should give you some advice. Tell you to rein it in a bit. Ruth is back today, by the way. Not a minute too soon either. The job hasn't been the same without her. I felt as if I was working with one arm tied behind my back."

"I enjoyed the christening. It was good to see the old team. Julian's done well for himself, hasn't he? He and Imogen make a grand couple."

"They're buying a house on that development where Zoe and Jo live. Can't be long now until they move in. That'll be the next bash — the house-warming."

* * *

Calladine entered the main office with a smile on his face. He was looking forward to having his partner back. Imogen and Rocco were great but they just weren't the same. The vibe was different. "Where is she then?" There was no sign of her and the morning was rattling on.

"Not arrived yet, sir. It'll be Harry. Ruth was saying only last week that he doesn't like nursery much. Howls the place down each time she leaves him," Imogen said.

"Poor little bugger. How old is he — six months?"

"It's a difficult decision. But I don't see Ruth as a stay-at-home mum, do you?"

Calladine shook his head. He knew Ruth would find it hard.

Imogen whistled. "Liking the suit, and the new look, sir."

Joyce cleared her throat and looked him up and down. "Looking good . . . DCI Birch wants to see you, said to tell you the minute you arrived. And DC Rockliffe has gone out on a shout."

"Anything interesting?"

"I'm not sure, sir. DCI Birch had a word with him and then he left."

"Did Birch say what she wants me for?"

"No — but she didn't look happy."

Calladine turned on his heel and made his way down the corridor. An unhappy Rhona Birch first thing on a Tuesday morning wasn't good. He hoped it was nothing he'd done. He wasn't in the mood for a bollocking. He knocked on her office door.

"Come in, Calladine. Sit down."

"You wanted to see me, ma'am?"

Her appearance was as severe as ever. A dark grey suit, buttoned-up shirt, short haircut and no make-up. But they were getting used to her. Rhona Birch had been with them a while now. She was okay in the main, but Calladine was still no nearer working out what made her tick. She was a closed book and her personal life a total mystery.

"First things first. We have a missing eighteen-year-old girl. DC Rockliffe has gone to speak to the family."

"Probably gone off in a huff. If we're lucky she'll turn up soon enough."

"Let's hope you're right. But that's not why I asked to see you. Take a look at this." She handed him a slim folder. "We've been asked to keep an eye out. This individual was released from Strangeways a couple of months ago. He's local. I see from the report that you know him."

Calladine looked at the image in front of him. "Craig Donnelly. Released! How did that happen? That piece of work was supposed to spend the rest of his natural life under lock and key. I worked on the investigation that put him away. Believe me, ma'am, it was no picnic." He shuddered. "Youngsters were his thing. He'd target some girl and make himself a damn nuisance. For months all we got were complaints. Until Annabelle Roper." He fell silent, his eyes fixed on the first page of the file. "It all changed with her. I was a sergeant at the time, working for DI Reynolds. He's retired now. Anyway, that case upset us both. Reynolds had to go off sick for weeks. I don't think I'll ever forget the way that girl looked when we found her." He flicked through the pages in the folder.

"Even after all this time it still makes very uncomfortable reading. Donnelly hacked her to shreds. She was almost unrecognisable. Annabelle Roper was a big girl, grossly overweight. Donnelly planned to put her in a wheelie bin and leave her for the rubbish collection. He couldn't make her fit so he used a cleaver to take off her limbs and her head. It was clumsily done. The pathologist reckoned she was still alive when he cut off her right arm. We found her naked, except for a school tie strung around what was left of her neck."

Birch frowned. "Not nice. Final cause of death? Blood loss due to having her limbs severed?"

"No." Calladine paused. The memory was painful and all too vivid. He didn't have to consult the file. What had been done to that girl had given him nightmares for weeks. "After removing her right arm, he cut out her tongue. She choked to death on her own blood. The rest of the cutting up was done post-mortem."

Birch's response was a single word. "Hobfield?"

"Oddly enough, no. He is from Lowermill, the Beech Lane development. It's at the top end of the village. The houses were built in the late sixties. Detached, large gardens — change hands for a packet these days."

"How did he afford to live there?"

"His wife had money. Her father was a surgeon. She is an accountant with a large firm. God knows what she was doing with him."

"Is he likely to go back to her? Did he and his wife stay together?"

"She dumped him the second he went inside, and who could blame her? But Donnelly is a mad bastard. He'll have scores to settle. One of those is bound to involve his ex-missus for not standing by him. He protested his innocence all through the trial. The papers even took up his case and ran with it for a while. But the evidence was all there. He was guilty alright." Calladine fell silent. Bad memories, some of the worst. "They had a child too. She must be grown up now."

"Gabrielle. She's seventeen."

"I don't understand what he's doing out. He killed a girl in the most awful way. He put her through hell, and now he's free. The judge at the trial said he was a danger to society. What happened?"

"Apparently he's a changed man. About five years ago he showed remorse. Accepted what he'd done. Then he got religion. Donnelly even studied for the clergy. Took exams, the lot. Some do-gooder priest supported and backed him. Now he's out on license, with a job and a place to live. All down to the church."

"Which church?"

"St James's in Leesdon."

"So now he's our problem."

"That depends on what he does and where he goes. I suggest you talk to the vicar, the Reverend Michael Livings."

Calladine was certain. "He's conned them. Don't ask me how because Donnelly's not that clever. It's taken a long time but he's worked out how to play the system. That bloody vicar, whoever he is, wants his head looking at. Religion, my backside! I bet Donnelly is laughing at the bloody lot of them. For our sakes and his, let's hope he keeps away."

"He may well want to see his daughter."

Calladine shook his head. "If she's got any sense, she'll refuse."

"Does he have any connection to this person?" Birch handed him a photo of a man wearing baggy clothes, with a full beard and long, untidy hair. It was impossible to guess his age.

Calladine squinted at the image. "Do you have a name?"

"He visited Donnelly in prison on several occasions over the last couple of months. He gave his name as Jason Kent. Of course that could be an alias. But he did produce ID. According to the visitor records, a passport."

"Could have been a fake," Calladine suggested. "They're easy enough to get hold of. If you know the right people."

"Donnelly didn't have any visitors apart from the official ones, and the vicar. Kent told the prison authorities that he was doing research for a book."

"What sort of book?"

"A book about murder, Inspector."

"Exactly how many times did he visit?"

"Six times in total. Always dressed the same. And he didn't interact with any of the other visitors."

"Significant, you think?"

Birch shrugged.

"Sorry, ma'am, I don't recognise him."

"Okay. Take the file with you and show the team. If Donnelly is seen in Leesdon with any undesirables or talking to young girls, let me know." She gave him a warning look. "And I don't want you approaching him. He'll scream police harassment, and that will give us no end of grief. Do you understand, DI Calladine?"

"Can't I mark his card?"

"No. Tell me. Uniform will keep an eye on him too. Unfortunately not this weekend though, they'll be thin on the ground. It's the Leesdon *Prom in the Park* on Saturday night, so they'll be mob-handed policing that little lot."

11

"I've seen the posters in town. We've not had one of those before. That'll keep them busy."

"That's what I'm afraid of. A couple of popular groups are attending. Not that I've heard of them," she added, making Calladine smile. "Local brass bands are playing too."

"An odd mix and not my cup of tea, but Leesdon Brass is worth a listen, ma'am. Does really well at the 'Whit Friday quickstep' most years."

"What on earth is that?"

Calladine chuckled. "Of course, you've not been around here long enough to have had the pleasure. It's a local brass band competition, ma'am. I say local, but the bands come from miles around. The idea is to compete in as many of the villages and towns as you can in one night. We get any number of famous bands rolling through here, clogging up the roads in their coaches. Brighouse, Black Dyke and Fodens take part regularly, as well as the local bands."

"A lot of effort has gone into organising this Prom thing. The money raised is going to the children's ward at the hospital."

"Very laudable, but it won't stop the villains off the Hobfield trying to cash in. They'll see it as a great opportunity to tout drugs and cause mayhem. It's asking for trouble, as far as I can see."

"I dare say you're right. But there's not a lot we can do."

That was the weekend up the spout. Uniform were good, but if anything serious went down it would be up to them. So much for time away with Shez.

"Check on the other team on your way back to the office. DI Long is on leave and Sergeant Thorpe is adept at dodging anything he doesn't like the look of." She nodded at the folder. "I've asked for some background on Jason Kent. Check where he's up to, would you?"

Calladine stood up to leave. Birch looked tired, even fed-up. "You had a trying few days too, ma'am?"

She sighed wearily. "Wore me out. As I'm sure you can tell from the way I look."

"If you need anything, the team are always happy to help."

"Thank you, but this is something I have to deal with myself."

She was giving nothing away. As Calladine went back to the main office, he wondered what that something was.

CHAPTER 2

"Will you drop Harry at the nursery?" Ruth Bayliss asked her partner Jake. She was running late. Night-time feeds, and a teething infant meant sleep was at a premium, so she'd not heard the alarm. A bad start to her first day back.

"Can't. Robert is struggling so I promised to meet with him early. We need to go over his lesson plans for today before classes start. He came to me on Friday asking for help and I can hardly refuse. We're only a few weeks into term, and I am supposed to be mentoring him. The life of an NQT is not an easy ride these days. Especially not with pupils like ours. The upper and lower sixth forms are merciless."

"Little buggers, the lot of them. Shame you can't just cuff 'em around the ear and be done with it."

He grinned. "It was the ruler across the palm in my day."

"Same here. Bloody hurt and all! But what about Harry?"

"Sorry, love." He pecked her cheek, and pinched the slice of toast hanging out of her mouth. "They'll understand down at the station."

Would they though? Calladine might, but Ruth already felt as if she was pushing it with the rest of the team. She'd extended her maternity leave by taking a few weeks' holiday that had been owing her. The team were short-handed as it was. They'd be counting the days.

How could she continue to be effective with all this baggage? And then there was Birch. Ruth had known things would change. It was how things were with babies. But this wasn't change — it was chaos. She was only one more setback away from sinking.

Moments later, Jake Ireson was out the door. Lucky him. Ruth looked around her sitting room at the mess. The sofa was stacked high with ironing. There wasn't a space on the floor that didn't have something of Harry's on it. There was loads to do before she could even think of leaving for work. Well, it would all have to wait. She hastily grabbed Harry's things and stuffed them into a bag. It would get better — had to. Her job didn't have regular hours so she'd have to rely heavily on Jake and the nursery to do the bulk of the childcare. With luck, Jake would sort out his newly qualified, and be a little more useful as the term moved on.

It had been a tough decision to put Harry in a nursery. But what else could she do? She needed to work. She loved her job. Without it, Ruth Bayliss would be a mere shadow of her true self. But Harry tugged at her heart so much she thought it would break. She was torn, and riddled with guilt, particularly when his little face lit up like a beacon each time he saw her. She told herself that plenty of other women did it. They worked full time and raised perfectly normal, well-adjusted kids. Plus, as Harry got older, he'd love the nursery. There were so many activities, and the staff were great with him.

As she pulled up outside the nursery, Ruth's mobile rang and her heart sank. It was Birch.

"Sergeant Bayliss, we missed you at the morning briefing."

Ruth knew that tone. Full of disapproval and undertones of *I hope this isn't going to be the norm*. She was late. Full stop. She'd try harder in future. She knew the score. Right now, Ruth didn't need Birch's reproaches.

"A teenager's gone AWOL from the Hobfield. One Elsa Ramsden. You may know the name. Family of rogues. DC Rockliffe has gone to have a word, but he's having difficulty getting a response from the house. He says they are in. Simply won't talk to police. Join him as soon as, and report back to DI Calladine."

Ruth was trying to pacify Harry who was screaming in his car seat. "On my way, ma'am. Sorry about the noise. I'm just about to drop him off."

"It is urgent, Sergeant. I don't want DC Rockliffe left on his own. An experienced eye is called for. This may be nothing, but we can't be sure." With that, she rang off.

Ruth cringed. That was all she needed — Birch on her back. This was what it would be like from now on. The constant juggling, the storytelling just so she could get by. Ruth wasn't sure she could do it. It was already wearing her down. Her mobile trilled to life again. This time it was DC Rockliffe, known as Rocco.

"Sorry, Ruth. I wouldn't have bothered you but Birch rang me and insisted. I'm trying to speak to the girl's mother but they're having none of it." His voice was shaky. "Bloody awful place. Top end of Circle Road. I'm not surprised Elsa's done one to be honest."

"Where's Calladine? Does he know?"

"He's got his medical with the doc this morning. I got the call before he got back. I've just spoken to Joyce, but now he's doing something for Birch. That's why I'm ringing you. I know it's not what you want on your first day back but . . ."

"It's okay, Rocco. Where are you?"

"I'm sat in my car, parked up opposite the house. I'll wait until you get here."

"Give me ten minutes. I'll just pop Harry into nursery and then I'll join you."

The noise of Harry bellowing away in his car seat was deafening.

"Doesn't sound as if he's up for it."

Rocco was chuckling, but he didn't have to deal with a screaming infant. "They tell me he's as good as gold once I've left. Apparently they're all like that."

"Rather you than me." Rocco rang off.

Grabbing Harry and his things, Ruth hurried to the entrance. It was already gone ten and she hadn't yet shown her face at work. Birch had every right to be annoyed.

"He's a lively one!" A young woman was walking up the path from the nursery in her direction.

"Lively at the very worst time. I'm late for work. I'm going to have to dump him and run."

"My Gemma used to be just the same. I shouldn't worry, they all come round in the end."

But Ruth had no time for chatter. She threw the woman a half-hearted smile and disappeared into the building.

* * *

You could set your clock by her. He liked that. She'd get up, have a quick shower, dress, do her hair, and add a little make-up. Then she'd be ready to log on promptly at eight for their daily date in cyberspace. She'd be sat on her bed in her school uniform, a smile on her face. He'd insisted upon this routine and she obeyed without question, wanting to please. And with good reason. She had suffered plenty of scathing comments during their virtual relationship. He was critical. He liked them a certain way.

"Wear your hair down, Megan. It doesn't suit you tied back, I've told you before." He watched the girl snatch the bobble from her ponytail. Her blonde locks fell like a curtain around her young face. Now she was beautiful. Young, lovely and blonde — his favourite type. He closed his eyes. He couldn't wait much longer. This one was the best so far. This one would be worth all the trouble, far better than her foul-mouthed friend. "That's much nicer."

A flush of pleasure reddened her cheeks. "You're still hiding from me. Why can't I see you for real?"

This again! They were never satisfied. He knew that plastered across her laptop screen was a picture of a young man with dark hair and a cute face. He had large brown eyes and a dimple on his right cheek. He'd chosen well. The image looked like a member of a boy band.

"My picture'll have to do for now. My computer's got some weird fault. Skype isn't working properly," he said. What matters is that I see *you*. I like looking at you, Megan." He watched her blush again.

"But I've never actually seen you properly. All I ever get is that photo. I wish we could meet up. This is okay, but it's no substitute."

Same old, same old. Why were they always like this? A few weeks down the line and it was all they went on about. Wanting to see him, to be with him. He couldn't have that. Cyberspace was all they would get — until the very last time. He closed his eyes, savouring the prospect. Soon it would be Megan's last time. She would be at his mercy, his very own, to do what he wanted with. He was almost ready. But not yet. He had to get rid of her friend first, she was stinking the place out. It wouldn't be long before people got curious.

"We talk, don't we?" he snapped at her. "It'll have to do for now. Tell me about last Friday. Did you do as I told you?"

She smiled proudly into the screen. "Certainly did. You were right, Gaby won't be so damn lippy now that we all know her little secret. You should have seen her face!"

"You told the others?"

"The whole class. None of them knew. She's a stuck-up cow, serves her right. The truth is she's no better than the rest of us. Her dad is a bloody jailbird. A murderer."

He smiled to himself.

She continued. "My friend's a gobby cow too. Word will soon get round. Elsa will tell the whole estate."

Not now, she won't. She's dead with no tongue. "You are very bad, Megan."

"Isn't that why you love me so much?"

He was silent.

"Want to know what else we did?"

"Go on."

She giggled. "Elsa took a sneaky photo of Gaby in the showers at school, after gym. Naked backside and all! It kept the class well entertained. She went ballistic. The head did too. Don't care though. It was worth it. We have her now, she'll have to do exactly what we tell her."

"You need to be careful. She might bite back."

"Not her, she's a pushover." She paused. "Your voice is funny. It always sounds weird, not normal like."

It wasn't. He had software on his computer to disguise it.

"Tell me, what are you going to do with the picture?"

"We'll blackmail the slag. She can keep us in dosh for the next few weeks."

"I have a better idea. Text it to all your schoolmates."

Silence. "Isn't that a bit much?"

"Don't question me, Megan."

"You can't tell me what to do!"

"Well, in that case perhaps we should re-think this whole relationship."

That hit the mark. Her face fell instantly and he could see the fear in her eyes. "I'll get into trouble at school."

"It will soon pass. Do it for me."

There was more silence, then, "Why do you live so far away?"

He closed his eyes, his patience was wearing thin.

"Because that's how it is."

He saw the frustration in her young face.

"Come and see me and I'll text the photo."

"Don't try to blackmail me, Megan."

Her face was flushed. He watched as she fiddled with her hair. He knew she wanted to please him, but she was wilful.

"Okay. I'll do it," she said at last.

* * *

Ruth tapped on the car window. "Rocco! Want to try talking to them again?"

"Sent me away with a gob-full when I tried earlier. I don't know how they expect us to find her if they won't give us the time of day," he complained.

"This whole thing's probably a waste of time. The Ramsdens have a bad reputation. And I recognise the girl's name." Ruth was skimming the missing person report. "Elsa Ramsden. She's one of Jake's sixth formers. He's spoken about her. She's a real handful, full of it. Gives the teachers a hard time. There's a gang of them, and she's one of the worst. A bully with a vicious streak. Not someone you'd cross. You'd think she'd know better being an A-level student. But supposing she really is in danger? Elsa is just the type to annoy the wrong person." She looked at the house across from where Rocco had parked. "That entire family are a nightmare. Come on then, let's give it another go."

Ruth rapped on the front door. While they waited, she cast a critical eye around the small front garden. It looked like a rubbish dump. Food wrappers, empty drink cans and an old mattress filled the small space. "This looks like the communal dustbin."

Rocco shrugged. "They're all the same down this street."

This time they had more luck. Mrs Ramsden yanked open the warped front door, swore, and gave both detectives a filthy look. She was small, with dyed blonde hair. Ruth put her in her mid-forties. She looked like a woman with a short fuse.

Mrs Ramsden began to speak before they'd even opened their mouths. "I know who you are, and before you start, we don't want no fuss. We don't want you speaking to people, neighbours and the like. It doesn't do round here."

Ruth attempted a smile. "A few questions about Elsa, that's all. Who her friends are, what she gets up to, that sort of thing."

The woman shrugged. "You're wasting your time. I know nowt. I do the best I can. I'm on my own with Elsa and three more. Lads, all teens, except Danny who's twenty-two. It was him went down the nick. Soft, he is. He worries. He kept on at me to report her missing. Waste of time. She'll be back when she's good and ready. It's easier just to let her get on with it. Elsa's a big girl now. I don't pry into her life, and she don't say much."

Ruth stopped smiling. "She's disappeared, Mrs Ramsden. Surely you want her found?"

The woman was dismissive. "It's Tuesday morning. She'll have gone to school."

"Have you checked?"

"No need. Elsa wouldn't miss. She's soft on that teacher of hers."

"Which teacher?"

"Mr Ireson."

Rocco gave Ruth a little grin, and asked, "When did you see her last?"

Mrs Ramsden folded her arms and blocked the doorway. "Friday morning when she left for school. You've been here long enough. People will see, and my boys won't like it. Elsa or no Elsa, I can't have the police tramping all through the house."

Ruth tried again. "I'm sure the boys'll want us to find Elsa too."

"The Ramsden crew have a reputation on this estate. Elsa will be fine. No one would dare do her any harm."

"Was anything bothering her, do you know?"

"Get real! That girl is every bit as bad as her brothers. The only thing she's got going for her is education. She's clever, and that teacher is good with her. Keeps her on track. She's got a shedload of GCSEs and she's doing A levels now." The woman shrugged. "Might do her some good. She's the only one of mine who's ever passed anything."

"We will speak to her teacher and her friends. If she turns up, or you think of anything else, ring me." Ruth handed Mrs Ramsden her card.

"She wasn't much help," Rocco complained as they walked back to the cars. "The kid's done one, or worse, and no one's much bothered."

"We'll look into it. I'll speak to Jake. He knows what goes on with the older kids at school. He might throw something into the pot."

Rocco smirked. "Elsa is soft on him then."

"Jake's got quite a fan club. Doesn't see it. I've told him to watch his step. Those girls are okay up to a point, but they can be lethal when they turn against you."

CHAPTER 3

It was lunchtime. He felt as if he'd been walking up and down the avenue for hours. She had to come back soon. He knew her routine, he'd been keeping tabs. She had no classes this afternoon.

Craig Donnelly checked his watch. Only an hour to go before check-in. Out on license — what a bloody laugh. He'd given those idiots in that prison everything they wanted. He'd been a model prisoner, saying and doing all the right things. The Reverend Michael Livings had put him straight. Explained what he needed to do, then coached him. He'd even started going to church. Finally they'd believed that he was genuinely sorry. Fools! If they knew the truth he'd still be under lock and key.

The bus stopped at the corner. She got off with a group of girls. Donnelly threw a cigarette butt into the gutter and craned his neck for a better look. She'd grown. When he'd got banged up, Leanne had been pregnant and Gaby was born two months into his sentence. Now she was a young woman, and so like her mother. Pity that. But at least her mother was a looker.

He stepped forward. "Gaby!" He hadn't been sure what to expect, but the look of horror on her face froze his soul. What had gone wrong? He watched and waited while she said a quick goodbye to her friends. "You got my letters? I wrote most days. And the photos? You must have. You recognise me?"

"Mum put everything you sent straight in the bin. I know what you look like because Mum showed me a recent photo. She warned me you might come calling. You're wasting your time! I hate you! I always have. Don't you dare come near me — understand?"

"But I'm your dad. I've missed you. I've counted the days. I've wanted to see you so bad."

"I haven't missed you. Not one bit, and who can blame me? Do you know how much trouble you've caused me and Mum over the years? The trouble you're still causing? Do you know that most of the kids at school don't want to know me anymore? Do you have any idea how that feels?"

His eyes narrowed. He knew exactly how that felt. If her life was so bad, how come she was refusing to have anything to do with him? All he wanted was to take her away from all this misery. "Whatever you think you know, it's wrong. It was all a big mistake. Things got twisted. People wanted me out of the way and I got banged up for something I didn't do," he said. "The authorities know that now, so they let me go. I'm out, aren't I? Would they do that if there were doubts? This is our chance to put things right. Put these mistakes behind us."

She took several steps backwards. "Don't come near me — creep. I don't want to breathe the same air as you! All my friends know what you did. Living in this town, going to that school, none of it is the same now. You ruin everything!"

"Don't say things like that, Gaby. I would never do anything to hurt you."

She screamed at him. "You exist, don't you? That's enough! Me and Mum want nothing to do with you."

The look of disgust on her face cut him to the quick. "But I'm your dad."

"You're a monster! A bloody embarrassment! Even more so now everyone's talking about you."

"It'll pass. People will soon forget. I can put it right. I have money. Why don't you come with me? We'll go away, somewhere warm. Have a holiday. I'll be a proper dad to you."

"Get lost!"

"I mean it, Gaby. I'll look after you."

"Mum looks after me. She always has. I go short of nothing. Look where we live." She gestured at the house. "Why would I give all this up to take off with someone like you?"

"I can talk your mum round, I always could. We can be a family again."

Gaby laughed. "Mum hates you even more than I do. When I tell her you've spoken to me, she'll go to the police."

He certainly didn't want that. "Okay, I'll go. But this isn't over. I want you in my life, Gaby. I'm not giving up."

* * *

Ruth put her bag and coat on the floor by her chair. Some welcome! Her desk was a shambles, covered in all sorts of rubbish. And only Joyce was in the office. No Imogen, no Calladine, not even any uniform. She nodded at the mountain of paperwork. "Where's that lot come from?"

Joyce cast her eyes over the untidy pile of documents. "Looks like the boss has lumbered you with the backlog."

Ruth picked at one or two pieces of paper. "It looks more like junk food central on here. Whiffs a bit too. This, for example." She threw a carton containing half a mouldy ham sandwich at the waste bin. "This paperwork is from months ago. Has Calladine been sitting here?"

"Eliza King had his office while she was here. The boss took your desk. He's been flitting between the two ever since. As for the rubbish — sorry. I think the others have been using your desk as a dumping ground."

"He doesn't do this with his own desk. Wait till he gets back! Where is he anyway?"

"He won't be long. He's sorting out Sergeant Thorpe. Imogen is down in records. I thought Rocco was with you."

"He was. He's getting some lunch in the canteen."

"I'll go through all that stuff," Joyce promised. "Stash it all on the shelves over there for now. Good to finally have you back, by the way."

Ruth smiled at her. "Good to be back. It makes me feel like life is becoming normal again."

"Got to have its compensations, though — a new baby, a spell at home. Not having to cope with everything that gets thrown your way here."

"It's felt really strange being away, Joyce. I like being a mum, but I like being a detective too. Don't ask me which I like best, cos I can't answer that. The roles clash. I'll just have to get used to it."

The two women heard whistling along the corridor and Calladine walked in through the office door.

A beaming smile crossed his face. "Aren't you a sight for sore eyes! Really glad you're back." He gave her a hug. "We've missed you, Ruth. All of us have."

"Glad to be back, boss. Although I could do without having to fumigate my desk!"

"Sorry — that's mostly down to me. Don't cope well without you, you see." Calladine winked at Joyce.

"Come off it. You're not a child."

"I've had to get by without my best sidekick. It's bound to tell in the end." Ruth looked him up and down. "Like what you see?"

"Not bad. Hairdo, new suit. A bit sharp for the office maybe. Who are you trying to impress? Last time I was here you looked a right state."

"Impress? Me? You're joking. But a bloke has to try. Apart from which, I had my run-in with the doc this morning."

Ruth had known Calladine was on something of a health kick, but she'd not expected him to stick to it. "You've really gone for it with the makeover. You look great."

"You don't look too bad yourself."

Ruth had her hands on her hips. "Never mind that. Plenty of time for compliments later. Now, what about all this clutter? Left to your own devices, you're hopeless, d'you know that? This desk is a disgrace. It doesn't look like you've done any paperwork for the entire time I've been away."

"I tried to keep up. But we've been pushed without you."

Ruth was smiling. "So you have really missed me?"

"Too bloody right. And you're back just in time. The work's building up. I couldn't stand having another unknown detective foisted on us. The last one was hard work, all attitude, and moody with it." He handed her the Craig Donnelly file. "Birch wants us to watch out for this character, but to keep a low profile. Problem is, I know him. He's an evil bastard I helped to put away years ago. It'll take more than a casual glance from uniform, or us, to keep him on the right track."

Ruth paged through the file. "Craig Donnelly? I've heard the name but I can't recall what he did."

"Teenage girls and young women — stalking, making a general nuisance of himself. Finally, he murdered someone. He got a long sentence. By rights he should still be inside, but he's been the model prisoner. Proper little governor's boy. So he's out on license. But the merest hint that he's up to his old tricks and his feet won't touch."

"And what's that?" Ruth nodded at the other file.

"Missing teenager."

"Elsa Ramsden? Rocco and I have just come from her home. Mother wasn't much help. More bothered about getting flak from the neighbours for talking to the police. Elsa is one of Jake's students. We will have to talk to him, and to her friends."

Back from lunch, DC Rockliffe came up to them.

"Rocco, set it up. Ring the school. Ask Jake to invite any parents who might want to be present at the interview. Impress upon him that we'll keep it low-key for now. Elsa might just have gone off in a strop after some row or other."

Ruth chipped in. "Coming from a family like that, it's highly probable. It was her older brother who reported her missing. Her mother doesn't seem bothered at all."

Calladine nodded at the file Ruth was holding. "She could have gone off with a boyfriend. We need to know a lot more about that young lady before we jump to any conclusions."

Ruth turned to him. "Did the doc keep you long this morning?"

"Did a right number on me, Ruth. A real going over. But he was pleased with the progress I've made. He still asked all sorts of tricky questions, though. Gave me all the chat about weight, booze and exercise. Given what I've achieved, it depressed me actually."

"Don't worry. He has to go on about all that stuff. They get paid to do it. He ticks a lot of boxes and job done."

Rocco put the phone down. "Jake says we can go to the school whenever we like. He confirmed that Elsa isn't in today, nor was she in on Friday or Monday. He also said that there had been a heated argument last week between Elsa and a Gaby Donnelly."

"Donnelly? Any connection to this chap?" Ruth waved the file.

"His daughter is called Gabrielle, so it could be her. She's the right age, and local."

"Her father is out. He has history with teenage girls. It might be jumping the gun, but perhaps we should pay him a visit."

"Let's see what her friends say first. If she hasn't run off to see some boy, and they don't know anything, then we will investigate what this Donnelly character has been up to."

"We need to do something. She's been missing since Friday morning and we've only just been told." Ruth checked the office clock. "Fancy some lunch first? It'll give Jake time to get the girls together."

"Okay, but I'm not allowed to eat much. You can tell me all your gossip."

28

Ruth grumbled away as they went down the stairs. "What gossip? For the last few months I've been a stay-at-home mum. I went to the baby clinic a lot. Got covered in sick more times than I care to think about, and I've hardly slept. You're the one with all the juicy stuff going on."

"That would be a reference to Shez, I suppose?"

"And why do you call her 'Shez?' What's her proper name?"

"Shelley. She's okay with Shell or Shez. It suits her. And yes, I suppose I do have a lot to tell. Not that I'm going to. I wouldn't want to make you blush." Calladine grinned.

"Come off it. You're showing off now. What I can't fathom is why she's with you in the first place. She's a lot younger, *and* she's good-looking."

Calladine protested. "I don't scrub up bad myself these days. New shape, new clothes, the hair. Could fancy me myself."

"You keep doing it, don't you?"

His reply was distinctly huffy. "Can't help it if women like me, can I?"

"She'll be after something. They always are."

"And here was me thinking I'd missed you."

"You have. I'm the voice of reason. You should listen. Go get us a table while I look at the specials board."

CHAPTER 4

Jake Ireson was in the sixth form common room, busy marking books. A group of chattering teenagers, a mix of girls and boys, sat at the back, their faces stuck in their phones, gossiping.

"How does he cope with this lot, Ruth? He deserves a bloody medal."

"At least they're not chucking stuff about or fighting. If they weren't texting or whatever, they'd be making a helluva racket."

Calladine looked round. "No parents. They all seem to have thought better of it."

Ruth nodded. "Work. Parents won't take time off for some spat at school. They'll expect the teachers to sort it out. Fortunately for us, that's okay. This is a group of eighteen-year-olds, so we don't need the parents."

Jake was sitting with a young man, ploughing through a pile of students' work. When he saw the two detectives he clapped his hands for silence. Several pairs of eyes swung their way, most eying Ruth with interest. Word must be out that she and Jake were an item.

Jake introduced the young man. "This is Robert Clarke, our latest recruit." There was a loud 'whoop' from the back of

30

the room. "Keep it shut, Rachel." Jake turned back to them. "He spends the majority of his time with this group, so I thought he should be here."

The look on the young man's face said he'd rather be anywhere than here.

Calladine turned to him. "Very brave, going into teaching. I couldn't do it. Not got the patience. I reckon it's worse than police work, the way teenagers are today."

Robert Clarke nodded but didn't say anything.

Jake shrugged. "This lot aren't that bad. We've had worse. What we've got here are the brains of the school. Most of them have their hopes set on university."

"Can I speak to them?" Calladine asked.

Jake nodded. He rapped on the desk with a text book. "Listen up you lot!" The group fell silent. They obviously knew better than to mess Jake around. "The inspector here is going to ask you some questions. Serious answers only, please."

"We've done nowt." The speaker was a blonde girl, sitting perched on the edge of a desk, filing her nails.

Calladine smiled. "I'm not saying you have. I just want to know about Elsa."

Another girl piped up. "Done one, has she? She'll be hiding from him." She giggled and pointed at Clarke. "Threatened her, didn't you, sir? You got all upset and sent for help. Called Elsa names. Swore a lot too."

Clarke flushed. "That's not true! I never even raised my voice."

"Calm down, Robert," Jake told him. "They're just having their few seconds of fun."

"At my expense as usual!"

"You're the new boy. They're testing the water, seeing how far they can push you. Take no notice. They'll get fed up soon enough."

"Was there an incident?" asked Ruth.

Jake shook his head. "No, this lot are taking the mick, as usual."

Ruth continued. "Does Elsa have a boyfriend?"

The blonde girl scoffed at this. "Not here. The lads in this school are too immature. Like bloody kids, the lot of them."

That brought a howl of protest from the boys in the group.

"Then who?"

The girl shrugged. "I dunno."

"Whoever it was, she spent her life texting or whatever. Never off her damn phone. Life would be a lot easier if the things had never been invented," Clarke added.

Ruth looked at the group. "So there was someone. Anyone going to tell us?"

The question was met with shrugs and muttering.

Calladine continued. "Was anything bothering her? Was she getting grief from someone?"

The group looked around at each other. More whispering.

Jake stood up and they all fell silent. "Okay, what is it?" He turned to Calladine. "I know this lot. You have to drag stuff out of them."

"There was that thing with Gaby last week. The photo, sir, remember?" Jake obviously had a lot more clout with the group than Robert Clarke. Now they might get somewhere, thought Calladine.

"Elsa, the girl who's missing, and Megan there," Jake nodded at the blonde girl, "took a photo of Gaby Donnelly in the showers after a gym session. Gaby was very upset. It was a back view but she was naked. Both girls were hauled in front of the head. The photo was deleted from Elsa's phone and they both apologised."

Ruth shook her head. "Gaby must have been angry and embarrassed, don't you think?" More silence. The students were looking at each other, as if afraid to speak. "Is Gaby here?"

They all shook their heads.

"So where is she?"

Robert Clarke intervened. "She said she had a headache and I let her go home. To tell the truth, I felt sorry for her. Gaby told me about her father. She was terrified that he'd try and contact her. She was really upset. What with him and the photo, she'd had enough. I hope I didn't overstep the mark, but I went to see her father. He is living nearby, at the vicarage. I asked him to stay away."

The blonde girl laughed.

"What is it, Megan?" Jake asked.

"Nothing, sir."

"Have you been upsetting Gaby again?"

She smirked. "No, sir. But you know how it is. Everyone's talking and pointing the finger. And it's no use speaking to her father, Mr Clarke. The man's just out of prison. Worse than that, he's a cold-blooded killer. He's not likely to listen, is he?"

Jake frowned. "Does the incident with the photo have anything to do with Elsa's disappearance?"

"No, sir."

"Are you sure? You are Elsa's best friend. If you know where she is, you should tell us. She won't get into trouble, and neither will you."

Calladine turned to the young man. "Mr Clarke, did you tell Donnelly about the photo?" Calladine was thinking that Donnelly would feel bad about not being around for his daughter. He might have tried to get even on her behalf.

"No, I didn't think I should," Clarke replied.

"It's got nowt to do with Gaby. She'll be with him, that bloke she sees. He likes her a lot. Takes her shopping in Manchester. Buys her stuff. She'll be back soon enough. Easily bored is Elsa," Megan said.

Calladine and Ruth looked at each other. "Which bloke? What's his name?"

"Some bloke she talks about. Friend of her brother, Danny. She really fancies him. Goes on about him all the time."

"Do you know where he lives?" asked Ruth.

Megan shook her head.

"Is it him she's always texting?"

Megan explained. "It's not texting we do, sir. We use a chat room. It's for students studying the same subjects. If we get stuck in class, we can get help. Go over stuff. Swap ideas, help each other with homework. Elsa used it all the time."

"A chat room? Is that allowed?" Ruth asked Jake.

"The students do use the internet for research. These days, that often means on their phones. It's a fact of life."

Ruth turned to Megan. "This boyfriend of hers, do you know his name?"

"Liam."

"Liam who? Is he local?"

"Like I said, he knows her brother. Danny will know."

Ruth handed Megan a card and a pen. "Write down the web address of this chat room for me. You need to check this out, Jake, make sure it's okay."

"I'd no idea they were using it."

"Let them go," Calladine decided. Megan handed Ruth the card and the students trooped out of the door.

Jake apologised. "They weren't much use. We still have no idea where she is. That chat room Megan talked about could be real or it could be a load of nonsense. That pair are as thick as thieves. They cover each other's tracks and get up to all sorts. Elsa is popular only with a small minority in the year group. Most of them give her a wide berth. She's clever, but trouble."

"I can second that," Clarke said emphatically.

Jake continued. "Gaby Donnelly annoys Elsa for some reason. I think jealousy is at the bottom of it. Gaby's mother is wealthy and Gaby has everything she wants. Elsa, as you'll know, is from the Hobfield."

"It will have been a big deal, the photo thing. If someone had done that to me, I'd be pretty cut up. I might want to get even," Ruth mused.

"Gaby is more level-headed than that. And the entire episode was nipped in the bud."

One of the pupils had returned, and approached Jake. "Sir?"

"What is it, Rachel?"

"That photo. Elsa did delete it, but first she texted it to Megan."

"So Megan has the photo on her phone now?"

Rachel nodded, and looked at the detectives. "Megan texted it to all her contacts. That means the entire sixth form and more."

Calladine groaned. Bloody kids! "Does Gaby know?"

"She must do. I think that's why she wanted to go home."

Ruth glared at Jake. "So much for nipping it in the bud! It would have been a good idea to make sure."

"These are older teenagers. In law they are adults. I can't take their stuff off them, Ruth. The head and I spoke to the group. We stood and watched as Elsa deleted it. What more was I supposed to do?"

"Be one step ahead! You know what this lot are like. You go on about them often enough at home," Ruth said.

Calladine wanted her to calm down. "It's not Jake's fault, Ruth. That girl who just gave us the information about the photo, what's her full name?"

"Rachel Hayes. She's a dark horse. Sometimes she's okay but she can also be every bit as nasty as the others," Clarke said.

"Do you know anything about this alleged boyfriend of Elsa's?" Ruth asked Jake.

"No, but she's not likely to discuss it with me, is she?"

"You could have overheard something. Girls talk."

"We'll ask her mother," Calladine suggested. Ruth was becoming agitated. She obviously thought Jake was far too lenient with the group.

* * *

Once they were outside and headed back to the car, Calladine reasoned with Ruth. "It's sixth form, not borstal. Jake is their teacher. I imagine it's challenging enough getting that lot through the exams. The truth is, he does wonders with them.

Leesdon Comp has a good success rate. I think he does a damn good job, given that the majority are from disadvantaged backgrounds."

"A woman would know what was going on. If it were me in there I'd have my finger on the gossip. I'd know who was seeing who. All that goes right over his head. He needs to keep an eye on Robert Clarke too. He's not coping. Jake left early this morning to help him with something. I bet those kids make mincemeat of Clarke in the classroom. Does Jake know the truth about that, I wonder?"

Calladine frowned. "This chat room the girls are using is worrying. They could be speaking to anyone. We need to get our hands on Elsa's computer, if she has one."

"Back to her mother's?"

"Okay. Then back to the station. We're going to have to speak to Gaby Donnelly. I don't like that particular connection."

"Neither do I." Ruth pointed. "The Donnellys live over there, other side of the park."

"Okay, a detour, a quick chat, then the station."

Ruth was struggling to keep up. "New thing, this walking everywhere."

"Part of my new regime. I try to get in as much as I can during the day, then a big walk with Sam once I've finished work."

Ruth was panting as they both came to a full stop outside the Donnellys' large stone residence. "Big house. Accountancy pays, doesn't it?

"Car's in the drive so they're home." Calladine knocked on the door.

Leanne Donnelly greeted them. She looked harassed. "Who sent the police? We haven't made a complaint. I wanted to, but Gaby thought it would only incite more awful behaviour from those girls."

"Is Gaby in?" Ruth asked.

"Yes. She couldn't stand being at school any longer. It's been non-stop. Heaven only knows why they pick on her. I don't understand it. Come on in."

The inside of the house was as impressive as the exterior. Gaby was in a sitting room at the back, playing with a small dog.

Ruth began. "We'd like to talk to you about Elsa Ramsden."

The girl stared at them for a few seconds, then her face crumpled and she burst into tears. "I hate her! She's a cow!"

"She's not a nice young woman, that's for sure," Leanne Donnelly added.

"I don't want to talk about her or Megan. You know what they did?" Both detectives nodded. "Not only did they show the entire class, they texted the damn thing to all and sundry! How do you think I feel?"

Ruth tried to reassure her. "We'll have a word with the school, Gaby, but for now, do you know where Elsa might have gone, or why she's disappeared?"

"No. But I hope she never comes back!"

Ruth nudged Calladine. "Your phone's ringing, guv."

Calladine fished it out of his jacket pocket. "Must be going deaf, as well as everything else."

It was Rocco. "We have a body, sir. Under Lane, far end of Park Road, leads down to the canal."

Calladine's jaw tightened. "Female?"

The line went quiet, then Rocco said, "Young too. I'm thinking . . ."

"Me and Ruth are on our way. Meet you at the scene."

* * *

The trees along Park Road had started to lose their leaves. After the recent rain they lay damp and limp on the pavement.

"Winter will be here before we know it." Calladine shivered. His expression was grim. He had been hoping for a runaway scenario, a touch of the Romeo and Juliets. Not this.

It was gone four, the schools were out and folk were making their way home from work. A crowd had already gathered. At the front, and craning his neck, was Robert Clarke. What was he doing here?

Ruth nodded towards the teacher. "Have you seen him?"

"He'll have got caught up in the crowd."

"He got here pretty fast, and listen to the buzz. They know it's a body. And he knows the girl."

The pair walked towards the cordoned-off area.

"I don't like this." Ruth gave a shudder. White-suited scenes-of-crime officers were swarming all over the area.

"Me neither. If this is Elsa Ramsden, it opens up a whole can of worms."

"Are you thinking of Gaby's father?"

"It's an angle we can't ignore. Gaby might have told him about the photo. We're going to have to speak to her again and ask her. He might have decided to get even on her behalf. A grand gesture, to make up for being absent most of her life."

Doctor Natasha Barrington from the Duggan Centre peeled the mask from her face. "Female, in her teens. The refuse collectors found her in that wheelie bin over there. Gave them a shock and a half! She's naked, apart from a Leesdon Comp tie around her neck with a name tag stitched onto the back. It reads 'Elsa Ramsden.' There is also a note fastened to the tie."

Calladine looked at Ruth. "Same MO as Annabelle Roper."

"Craig Donnelly is looking like our best bet then."

"We'll see. There were details about Annabelle's death that were never released. It could be a copycat."

"Where's the body now?"

"We're just doing the recovery," Natasha Barrington replied. "It isn't pretty, Inspector. She's been dead about forty-eight hours, and in the bin for roughly half that time I'd say. I'm afraid the flies have been at her. Plus, there is what's been done to her hand and mouth. Your DC Rockliffe threw up. He's over there."

Calladine had never forgotten Annabelle Roper. If this was the same killer, he knew exactly what would have been done to Elsa. The details had sickened him then and it would be no different now.

"Hand looks like it's been deep fried, does it?" He hadn't meant to say that. *Deep fried*! It was a hand for goodness sake, not a helping of chips!

"Yes, exactly that." Natasha Barrington looked at him. "You've seen something like this before, Inspector?"

"Unfortunately. The victim in the case I'm thinking about had a badly burned hand. It had been deliberately done. That was just for starters."

"There is very little flesh left. The fingers have been burned down to the bone."

Ruth was beginning to feel sick.

"Her mouth — is the tongue missing?" asked Calladine.

Natasha nodded. "Cut out far back too. She was alive when it was done. At this point I'd say that she choked on the sheer volume of blood. Her mouth was sealed with black tape. Although it wasn't pulled tight, the tie around her neck won't have helped either. The blood will have had nowhere to go. Some will have escaped through her nose. The rest — it would have choked her."

Calladine cleared his throat. "The note. I'm guessing two words."

She nodded again. "Yes, Inspector. The note has *Dead Meat* scrawled across it."

Calladine exhaled. "In that case, it's no copycat. Apart from those working on the case at the time, only one other person knew what had been done to Annabelle Roper. Or what the note said."

"The perpetrator?"

"And he got out of Strangeways recently."

She held out her hands, as if to say 'well there you are.' "We'll get what we can forensically. If it is your man, his DNA will be on file."

"We need that computer from Elsa's home urgently, as well as her mobile phone and any other technology she owns."

"I can see to that." Still a little green around the gills, Rocco joined them.

39

"Okay, I'll leave that with you. Take Imogen and a uniform with you. Volatile lot the Ramsdens, so tread carefully. You've seen the body. Ask to see a photo of Elsa before you launch in and tell them she's dead."

"If it's her, do I tell them the truth, sir?"

"Just that Elsa has been murdered. None of the detail. Arrange for family liaison to go along too. I don't reckon their chances much, but you never know."

"We've searched the area and haven't found any of her belongings. Certainly no phone," Natasha Barrington added.

"Rocco, when you're speaking to the Ramsdens find out who Elsa's service provider was. When you're back at the nick get a list of calls, texts and anything else that phone has been used for."

Calladine's face was drawn. He looked at Ruth. "We'd better go have a chat with Craig Donnelly." He beckoned to a uniformed officer standing nearby. "Get rid of this lot, will you? A bunch of bloody ghouls."

"That includes Clarke?" Ruth asked.

Calladine ignored the question. "We'll take a car this time. Donnelly's staying at St James's with the vicar. He's the do-gooder who helped get the bastard released."

* * *

St James's church was an early-Victorian monstrosity. Along with the grounds, graveyard, vicarage and the cottage Donnelly lived in, it covered a large area that bounded Leesdon Common. Numerous Leesdon historical worthies rested in the graveyard. The most elaborate stonework, and at least one of the family vaults, belonged to wealthy cotton mill owners who'd lived and worked in the Leesdon area. But these days many of the ornate gravestones had collapsed, battered by the weather. The predominant colour was black, from the days when everyone in Leesdon burned coal in their fireplaces. The word that sprung to Calladine's mind was 'grim.' Of all the churches in Leesdon, this one was the least attractive by far.

The Reverend Michael Livings was not at all pleased to see the two detectives standing in his doorway. "Can't leave him be, can you? Craig has done his time and paid his penance. He's a different man now. He deserves some peace and quiet."

Calladine pocketed his badge. "Ordinarily I'd agree, vicar. But we have a problem." He watched the man fold his arms and tap his foot irritably against the step. "You recall Annabelle Roper? The young girl that Donnelly was put away for murdering?"

Michael Livings was a very tall man. He towered above Calladine. He stuck his long nose in the air and his dark eyes were pinpoints of rage as he looked down on them.

Calladine ignored the body language. "Our problem is that it's happened again. And soon after Donnelly was released."

"This is harassment."

"This is the law going through due process. Me doing my job. Donnelly's MO — method of killing, that is, was unique. In all the years I've been doing this job, I've not seen a case like it. Now we have another." Calladine met the man's stare. "You have to agree, it's an odd coincidence."

"And that is what it will be, Inspector, coincidence. One dead girl and the first thing you do is beat a path to his door. How is the man supposed to make a fresh start? How does he put the past behind him? Craig knows he did wrong back then, but he is a changed man now. He will not repeat his actions. He has sworn as much to me, on the Holy Bible, Inspector!" He added, "And I believe him!"

Calladine replied evenly, "More fool you. Personally I wouldn't believe anything the murdering bastard said. But each to his own." The vicar's tone was beginning to grate.

"He isn't here," continued the vicar. "If you bothered to check you'd know that Craig sees his parole officer on alternate mornings."

Ruth raised her eyebrows. "That's pretty frequent. Frightened he'll do a runner?"

"No, of course not. Craig has every intention of doing the right thing. It is a condition of his licence."

Calladine was amazed. Michael Livings might be a vicar, doing good and all that, but surely he could see what was staring him in the face? "You really have been duped, haven't you? A man like you, who is supposed to have a grasp of the human condition! Can't you see what he is doing? He's conned you, vicar, he is as guilty as sin. I hope you can live with yourself if it turns out he has killed this girl."

"He is truly sorry for what happened all those years ago. Craig Donnelly has it in him to be a good man. He simply needs the opportunity. He helps out around the church, and in return I provide him with the small cottage at the back of the vicarage. I have come to know the man and I will not change my opinion on the say-so of some embittered copper who can't see further than the end of his nose!" With that, the vicar banged the door shut.

Ruth almost smiled. "Well, that told you. He was very helpful."

"We are going to have to search that cottage, Ruth."

They made their way back to the car. "I agree, but make sure all the paperwork is watertight first. That vicar is a strange one. He looked a bit odd too. Not like a man of God at all. There was something almost evil about him. He reminded me of that actor that used to be in all those horror films way back when. You know — the tall, thin one."

But Calladine wasn't listening. He'd just spotted Craig Donnelly dodging behind a hedge. He pointed. "Go that way so he doesn't disappear onto the High Street. I'll follow him."

Craig Donnelly nipped into the churchyard via a gap in the rear fence. Calladine moved fast and was on his tail in seconds. He grabbed hold of the man's jacket just in time to stop him disappearing into a side door of the church.

Calladine hauled him back. "Not so fast, mate."

Donnelly cowered, covering his face with an arm. "Don't hit me!" he yelled.

"Why not? I'm sorely tempted to kick your stupid head in, you evil piece of shit!"

After nearly twenty years, Calladine was again face to face with the murderer. He saw Annabelle Roper stuffed into that bin, along with bits of her body, like pieces of a human jigsaw puzzle. This man was responsible for doing that to a young girl. He should not be walking the streets.

"Leave me! Leave me alone! You can't do this."

Calladine looked at the terrified man. He was aching to lamp him one across the jaw, knock him to the ground and stamp the life out of the murdering bastard.

Then Ruth ran up to him. "Tom! You've got him."

Ruth was glaring at him, and her look told him not to go too far. Calladine's grip relaxed. He caught his breath. "We need to have a serious chat, Craig Donnelly. Down at the station."

"You can't do this! I'm clean, just come back from seeing my probation officer. I've got a job, a place to live, so shove off, copper!"

Calladine showed him his badge. "It won't take long."

"You're picking on me. I haven't done anything other than work for that slave driver," he nodded at the vicarage. "I know who you are. You were one of the coppers that put me away. You got it all wrong then and you're doing it again now."

Calladine ignored this. "We want to know exactly where you've been and who you've spoken to over this last week. So you can get your thinking cap on while we tootle off to the nick."

"You can't make me come with you."

"Yes, we can, Craig. If necessary, I'll arrest you."

CHAPTER 5

Elsa Ramsden's mother stared at them. "What d'you mean —
a photo of Elsa? What do you want it for?"

Rocco tried to smile. "Something recent?"

She gave a puzzled shrug and snatched a framed picture
from the wall behind her. "This is her. Happy now?"

There was no doubt. The dead girl was Elsa Ramsden.
Rocco passed the photo to Imogen with a little nod.

"Can we come in, Mrs Ramsden?" Imogen asked.

"Why? What do you lot want now?"

There was no easy way to say this. "We'd like to talk
about Elsa. I'm afraid she's been murdered."

The woman's eyes flitted wildly from one detective to the
other and she gave a nervous little laugh. "This is someone's
idea of a bad joke. She's at school. I told his mate that not long
ago." She nodded at Rocco.

Imogen spoke kindly. "Elsa isn't at school, Mrs Ramsden.
She was found earlier today. I'm afraid she's been murdered."

Elsa's mother shook her head. "You're wrong. No one
would hurt our Elsa. Wouldn't dare."

"She's been missing since Friday. Why didn't you report
it?" Rocco asked.

Mrs Ramsden was dismissive. "She's always taking off, but she comes back. And she will this time, you'll see."

"Can we come inside, Mrs Ramsden?" Imogen asked again.

This time Elsa's mother moved aside and gestured down the narrow hallway. "Last night her eldest brother, our Danny, got a bit bothered. He went looking for her. He ended up going down the nick and telling them how long she'd been gone. Truth is, I wasn't worried. She's always staying with that friend of hers."

"Megan Heywood?" Rocco asked.

"Yes, her. Them two are always together." Suddenly their words seemed to hit home. Tears began to trickle down her face. "You'll have got this all wrong. I can't lose my Elsa. Megan will tell you what happened. Go and see her. My Elsa will be with her, you'll see."

Imogen introduced their colleague. "This is a family liaison officer. She will keep you up to date with everything that happens."

But Mrs Ramsden was adamant. "I don't want no police in the house."

"In that case can we get someone else for you? A relative, perhaps?"

"Look here, missy. You lot have got this all wrong. Our Elsa will come skulking through that door anytime now. She'll tell me what she wants for her tea, then she'll go straight up to her room."

Imogen looked at Rocco. "No she won't, Mrs Ramsden. Where can we find your son, Danny?"

"He'll be in the bookies on the High Street. But there's no need to disturb him. Go and see her friends first. Megan or one of the others will know where she's hiding."

"We will be speaking to Megan later. Meanwhile, we need to take Elsa's computer and her mobile, if it's here. We have to take it away so that our people can look for anything on it that might help. Once they're done, you can have it back," Imogen said.

Imogen waited for Mrs Ramsden to refuse point-blank. But nothing happened. Without so much as a word, the woman flopped onto the well-worn sofa. The awful news was finally sinking in.

She sniffed. "Her room's top of the stairs, first on the left. Help yourselves. But you won't find her mobile. That's glued to her hand."

Imogen looked at Rocco. "We didn't find it with her."

"Does she have a tablet?" asked Rocco.

"No. It was all I could do to buy her the laptop."

The house was scruffy. The stair carpet was threadbare in places and the paintwork was chipped. The door next to Elsa's looked as if someone had had a go at kicking it in at some time.

They opened the door to Elsa's room. It was surprisingly large and looked like a little palace. She had a double bed with a cream lace canopy and pink fairy lights draped around the headboard. The furniture was old, but it had been carefully painted in a delicate pink. The wallpaper was covered in butterflies and she had curtains and bedding to match.

Rocco smiled. "Very girlie."

Imogen nodded. "This isn't the Elsa Ramsden I was expecting from what we've heard of her. But it's nice, pretty. I like it."

Rocco picked up the laptop from the dressing table. "We should get this over to the Duggan, pronto. If there's anything to find, their IT people will be on it like a shot."

Elsa's mother stuck her head round the door. "She could be all night on that thing. Spends hours up here she does, talking to some boy or other. Heard him once. Swanky accent. Sounds like he has money. Can't understand what the poor bugger sees in our Elsa."

Imogen raised an eyebrow. "Did she ever talk about him?"

"Not to me she didn't. Megan's your best bet on that one."

"How long has it been going on, the thing with this boy?"

"Who knows? She comes up here, locks the door. Plays holy hell if her brothers go near."

"Have you never asked her about him?"

"Wouldn't get me anywhere if I did. I don't have time to play games with Elsa. She wants me to know something, she'll tell me. Otherwise I leave her to it. If you take the laptop away, make sure it comes back. I'm still paying for it."

Once they were outside, Rocco said to Imogen, "I don't think she understands. And what about the identification?"

"We can't ask her. The girl's mouth is a mess." Imogen thought for a moment. "We'll go and find the brother."

* * *

"I explicitly told you to leave him alone, and to report back to me."

Calladine was back in Birch's office, and she was livid. Her small, dark eyes were slits. "I have my orders too, you know. Now I'm going to have to explain to the assistant chief constable what Craig Donnelly is doing in our cells!"

"He's a suspect—" But Calladine didn't get a chance to explain.

"A suspect! What do we suspect him of, for God's sake? I hope you've got something good up your sleeve."

"I certainly have, ma'am. But I don't understand why the ACC would want him leaving alone."

"That's not the issue. The issue is that you blatantly disobeyed an order."

"Sorry, ma'am, but I had no choice."

"Why did you bring him in? I need something concrete to tell the ACC or it'll be both our careers down the pan."

Calladine's smile was half-hearted, and he just stopped himself shrugging. His career had gone down the pan a long while ago. His association with the villain, Ray Fallon, had seen to that. "The dead girl, ma'am. It has all the same hallmarks as the Annabelle Roper case. There are injuries present that were never released to the press or anyone else at the time. This victim, Elsa Ramsden, has them all."

That got her attention. "Donnelly was carefully monitored for years. His prison record is spotless. He expressed remorse for what he did. So why do it again within weeks of getting out? He received counselling and treatment, and finally became a trusted inmate. I'm at a loss to understand what happened, particularly with the system."

Calladine grimaced. "I wouldn't waste time trying to work it out. I think someone a lot cleverer than he is coached him on how to play the system. The victim is known to Donnelly's daughter. Elsa Ramsden was giving Gaby Donnelly grief at school. Perhaps Craig decided to get even as some sort of grand gesture."

"His family want nothing to do with him, so how would he know?"

"I've no idea, but I intend to question him. I want to know how he has spent his time this last week, who he's seen and where he's been. Given the nature of the killing, surely even the ACC can't complain at what I've done?"

"Okay, speak to Donnelly. But do it by the book. Make sure he has legal representation, contact his probation officer and see if he wants to be present too. I don't want any comebacks. Do you understand, Calladine?"

"Perfectly, ma'am."

"I take it forensics are on the job?"

"The merest speck of Donnelly's DNA and we'll have him."

* * *

Once he was back in the incident room, Calladine went over to Ruth. "Why do you think the ACC would want to keep Craig Donnelly sweet?"

She looked up from a file she was busy reading. "What d'you mean?"

"Birch told me to leave him alone. To report, not act. She's pretty damned annoyed that I've just arrested him. Apparently it goes against what the ACC wants."

Ruth tapped a pencil against her front teeth, then she nodded. "It won't be Donnelly, it'll be that vicar. Bet I'm right. They'll have some connection and the vicar'll be leaning on the ACC. You met the man, would you want him on your back?"

Calladine smiled. "Check it out. If you are right, you get a gold star."

"Where do I start? I can't just go prying into the ACC's private life."

Calladine thought. "Who have we got at the moment anyway?"

"Patrick Kennet."

"Now that is interesting."

"Not really. I've never met the man and I'm not likely to either."

"I have," Calladine told her. "At the time he was DCI Kennet, working from Oldston station. He supervised the investigation into the Annabelle Roper murder."

"You and Reynolds worked with him, then?"

"Not me. I met him a couple of times tops, but he drove Reynolds crazy with his demands."

Ruth frowned. "So what does it mean?"

"Probably nothing. Look at the vicar instead. Speak to some of the parishioners first. See what Livings is into, whether he's a member of any societies or clubs. You can check if the ACC belongs to the same ones."

"Would Birch know?"

"I'll ask, but I doubt it."

Calladine's mobile rang. It was Doctor Natasha Barrington from the Duggan. "If I were you I'd get myself a cup of hot, sweet tea and sit down."

"Bad, eh?"

"One of the worst I've had in some time. I don't say this often, Tom, but this character needs catching, and quick. Before he gets a taste for it."

The tea wasn't a bad idea. Calladine looked at Ruth. "Any chance of a cuppa? Doctor Barrington is about to relay something nasty."

Ruth went to the brew corner, grabbed the kettle and went off to fill it.

"I'd say the sequence of events went something like this . . ." Natasha was wasting no time on small talk. Calladine could hear the edginess in her voice. Natasha Barrington had had Elsa on the table for a couple of hours by now. She'd have done the preliminary examination, so she'd be well aware of what the girl had suffered. What she'd found had obviously got to her.

"She was kept tied up for a while and drugged regularly — morphine I'd say, but I'm still running tests. Apart from the other injuries, her lower arms are red and inflamed. I'd say she was allergic to whatever tape was used to bind them. Her hand was burned first, and it's no superficial burn either. It went down to the bone. I will await the results before I say for sure how that was done. Despite the drugs, the poor girl would have been in agony. She'd have lost consciousness at this point." She sighed. "But he didn't stop there. Elsa has scratches and grit embedded in the skin of her back and buttocks. She appears to have been lying naked on rough ground. Bruises to her face and upper body suggest she was beaten. And while she was still pinned down, Elsa was raped."

"Was she conscious?"

"Given the morphine in her system, hopefully not. I haven't run all the tests yet so that is still conjecture at present."

Calladine's head was reeling. Ruth put the tea on the desk in front of him, and he grabbed it and took a swig. "Poor kid. The bastard really went to town! What I don't understand is why."

But there was more. Natasha went on. "He jammed her mouth open with something large and hard. She has two broken teeth, top front. He pinched her nose tight shut with something. I've found tiny flecks of black paint. For the time being I'm going with a bulldog clip. There is evidence of extensive bruising to both sides of her nose. And then he cut out her tongue. Elsa was lying on her back. He used something sharp, a knife or scissors. When that was done her mouth was taped up. She would not have lasted long. She would have choked to death on her own blood."

There was a moment or two of silence. Eventually Calladine asked, "Did you get any DNA?"

"No."

"He did all that to the poor girl and left no trace? How is that possible?"

Natasha spoke as if it was obvious. "He was forensically aware. A lot of people are nowadays. They watch too much telly and have learned what not to do. The suits, the gloves and masks, they're all readily available and cheap to buy. He even used a condom."

"Anything about the body give any clues as to where all this took place?"

"Possibly, but you'll have to wait for that. I've passed everything over to Professor Batho, including the note. It is smeared with blood. I'm having some of her hair tested. It is long and matted with dried blood but it may have picked up something. I'm thinking spores, or mould, from where she was held, even the odd specimen of wildlife."

"Wildlife?"

"Fleas, flies, maggots, rat droppings. She was found in a dustbin, Tom. We've also handed the other contents over for analysis. I'll keep you informed." Her sigh was loud. "I'm beginning to wonder why I do this job."

"You and me both. However, I do have a suspect in custody. As I told you, I have seen this before. The bastard is in the cells. I'll let him stew and then go and have a word."

"Give him a damn good thumping for me, will you?" Then Natasha went silent.

"You alright, Tash?"

"No, I'm bloody not! She was just a girl. A teenager, with her whole life ahead of her. It's not often the job gets to me, but this one has tipped the balance."

"Perhaps it's you that needs that tea."

"It'll take more than tea. You doing anything tonight?"

CHAPTER 6

Birch's voice reverberated around the room. "Calladine! A word in my office."

Calladine got up and followed the DCI. "If I'm not out in ten, come and rescue me," he whispered to Ruth.

"You need to do something about Donnelly fast. I've had the ACC on. In turn he has had the Reverend Michael Livings on his back. You didn't just arrest him, did you? You frightened the life out of Donnelly. He is threatening to make an official complaint. Have the Duggan come up with anything yet?"

Calladine shook his head.

"You have no evidence to back up dragging him in here. No witnesses, no DNA, a big fat nothing, bar your suspicions."

"It'll take time, ma'am. The Duggan are working on the case as we speak."

"We don't have time. We can't hold him. Livings and the probation officer are on their way here now to collect him."

"How did they find out so fast?"

"Donnelly rang Livings. He arranged a solicitor." Birch shrugged. "A solicitor who knows his stuff. You were violent."

Calladine protested. "I never touched him! I wanted to, but Ruth stepped in just in time."

53

"You're damn lucky she did, or you would be out on your ear. What has got into you, DI Calladine?"

"This is a horrific killing, ma'am. I've just had the preliminary report verbally from Doctor Barrington. Imprisonment, torture, the burning of her hand, rape and finally a brutal death. Donnelly has history. The details of Elsa Ramsden's and Annabelle Roper's murders are very similar." He paused. Birch was listening, but her attention had wandered. She was staring at the mobile phone on her desk as it blinked away silently. "What am I supposed to do?"

She shook her head. "Your job, Inspector. Wait for the evidence. Until you have something positive against Donnelly, go and harass some other suspect."

"There are none."

"Perhaps that's where you're going wrong." She sighed, finally picking up the phone. "I'm going out shortly. The chances are that I won't be here when Livings arrives. Treat him with kid gloves. Do you understand?"

Calladine nodded.

"Find out where Donnelly has been. Chase up everything he gives you. I have made it clear that he will be released into the vicar's care, and he has promised that Donnelly will not do a runner."

"Am I allowed to speak to him first, ma'am?"

"Yes, but for pity's sake don't upset him."

* * *

"Bloody good, isn't it? We have a convicted killer and I'm supposed to pussyfoot around. Anyone would think that he was some sort of VIP." Calladine said to Ruth as they made their way down to the interview room.

"While you were in with Birch I made a couple of enquiries, and they paid off. It's the golf club. Both the ACC and Livings are members and they play together regularly."

Calladine couldn't believe it. "And that's it? They're golf buddies, so Donnelly walks?"

"I'm still checking, but it's a start. At least we've ascertained that they do know each other."

"There's got to be more to it than that. The ACC is no fool. He wouldn't put his job on the line for a game of golf." Calladine shook his head.

Craig Donnelly's solicitor sat with him in the interview room. He was a tall man in an expensive suit, clutching a voice recorder. Whoever had hired him was obviously willing to pay through the nose.

Calladine pasted a smile on his face. "Craig. Sorry to drag you away from your work, but you know how these things are. I'd like to ask you a couple of questions. You okay with that?" Calladine looked at the two men. Donnelly nodded, and the solicitor said nothing. "Can you tell me what you've been doing over the past week?"

"That's a lot of time, Inspector, and I'm a busy man." For a moment Donnelly seemed to be thrown by this request. His eyes flicked around the room from one person to the next, as if seeking the answer. Then his face suddenly brightened. "But you're in luck." He nodded at his solicitor, who opened his briefcase, pulled out a notepad, and handed it to Calladine.

"Fortunately my client has kept a list. Dates, times, places, and the names of people who can corroborate what is written there."

Calladine scanned the pages. Donnelly had made copious notes about his day-to-day life since leaving prison. It was all there. Almost as if he'd expected to be dragged in like this and had prepared. "You've done your homework. I'm impressed." Calladine tapped the book. "So if I go and speak to . . ," he chose a name at random, "Charles Walker, he'll confirm you were cleaning his windows the day before yesterday. Is that right?"

Donnelly nodded. "I've spent most of my time ministering to the needs of the reverend's flock. Charles Walker is eighty-two. He can't manage his windows on his own. After sorting him, I dug over Mildred Owen's potato patch. Kept me until gone nine that night, she did."

"Regular pillar of the community, aren't you?"

"I'm doing my best. I'm trying to make up for the past. I owe this community a debt for taking me back. I'm grateful."

Was he for real? Calladine shook his head. He didn't believe a word of it.

The solicitor looked at his watch. "I'm sure you don't want a blow-by-blow account of what's written down there, Inspector. Keep the notepad, check what you will, but in the meantime I must insist that my client is released."

"Okay," Calladine said simply. "But don't leave town."

Calladine had not expected this. Notes, witnesses that could be checked. Livings really was taking good care of Donnelly. But why? Couldn't he see what was staring him in the face?

Michael Livings loomed at the end of the corridor as they exited the room. "Inspector! This really is bad form."

"Just doing my job, reverend," Calladine said.

The man stood at the vicar's side thrust a hand the DI's way. "Joe Rushton, Craig's probation officer. Craig hasn't put a foot wrong since he got out. I see him several times a week. You've seen the diary, it's all in there."

Calladine nodded. "Good idea that. We'll start working through it."

Michael Livings gave him a hawkish stare. "Keep off our backs, Inspector. I will report you to your seniors if we have any more of this harassment."

With that, Livings nodded at Donnelly and they walked off towards the exit.

"What now?" Ruth asked.

"We'll go and have a word with Megan Heywood. See what she has to say for herself. Get her address and meet me at the car. I want another word with Birch."

* * *

He walked back to the DCI's office door and was about to knock, but heard her arguing with someone on the phone. From what she was saying, it wasn't about work. It sounded personal. She was speaking to someone she called Reg. Calladine turned and walked away. Birch hadn't looked right for a day or two. The woman had something eating at her. Ordinarily she'd have been one hundred percent on his side when it came to sorting Donnelly. The fact she'd given in so easily to Livings spoke volumes to Calladine. Rhona Birch had something serious going on in her private life.

"Megan Heywood lives on the Hobfield. Down the road from Elsa," Ruth told him as he climbed into the car.

"How does Birch seem to you?"

"Can't say I've had much to do with her since I got back. Why?"

"She's not right. She's got stuff on her mind, and it's influencing the job. In fact it's playing havoc with her judgement."

Ruth gave him an odd look. "Your judgement has been a little off-beam too, while we're at it."

"In what way?"

"Your certainty that Donnelly is guilty of this new crime."

"I'm certain because I'm right. I want every single entry in that notebook checked. I want to know exactly what that bastard has been up to since he got out."

Ruth frowned. "I've been looking at the Annabelle Roper case."

"And? Spot anything interesting?"

"Donnelly protested his innocence all the way. Through all the interviews, during the trial, and later when he was banged up. He never stopped. That only changed when he met Livings."

"What are you saying, Ruth? That Livings has some magical power that made Donnelly finally see the light and repent?"

"No, but until Donnelly did admit what he'd done and show remorse, he was never getting out. Up until that point he had been a pain in the arse. Always in fights, always screaming about being innocent. Meeting Livings changed all that."

"You think finally admitting he was guilty was a deliberate move?"

"Yes, I think it was. Livings coached him. He took Donnelly under his wing. Despite the rich wife and the big house, Donnelly was all Hobfield. A bit of a scally, a bit too fast with his fists when he'd had a skinful, but up until the Roper case he'd never been in any real trouble."

Calladine could hardly believe his ears. He turned onto Circle Road and pulled into the first available space. "Are you saying you actually think Donnelly could be innocent? What about the other young women he bothered? Can't you see the pattern?"

"No, not really. I think that was all circumstantial."

Calladine's voice was flat. She'd shaken him. "There was sound forensic evidence, Ruth. Including a necklace belonging to Annabelle, found in his house. And her blood was found on one of his shoes. He insisted he'd never even met her. So how did that happen if he was telling the truth?"

"I don't know. But there was other stuff that didn't add up. Annabelle had told her friend that she was being stalked. The description she gave to the police could have fitted most men in Leesdon! The local rag got wind of it and several other women came forward. That was where the idea that the stalker had to be Donnelly came from. Eventually a description of the man was cobbled together. But still there was no consensus. One said he was blond, another that he was bald! But Donnelly got labelled the 'Leesdon stalker,' and the rest you know."

Calladine was struggling. How come she'd seen all this? He'd worked the case, lived it, suffered all the sleepless nights. "I can't believe you of all people could be swayed like this. Vicar or no vicar, that bastard is as guilty as sin. And I'm going to prove it!" He paused, his gaze fixed on the road in front of him. "I need you with me on this, Ruth. We are a partnership. We have our differences, and that's healthy in a job like ours. But on this one we have to stand together."

He could see that Ruth was uncomfortable. "It's not that simple, Tom. There are differences between the murders. I can't pretend they're not there, and neither can you. There was no rape in the Roper case for example. Neither was her mouth taped shut after her tongue had been cut out. Plus all her clothes, bar that necklace, were found with her body in the bin."

Calladine took a deep breath. Ruth was right.

CHAPTER 7

Rachel was speaking to the image on her laptop screen. "I didn't think you'd noticed me. You were so into Elsa, then Megan. I left messages, but you never replied."

There was a slightly distorted chuckle. "I noticed you alright, Rachel. Megan was a mistake. She's a real bore so I'm dumping her. Apart from which, you are much prettier."

Rachel Hayes blushed at the compliment. "Are you going to tell her it's over?"

"No, I'm going to leave that to you. And don't be kind about it. Tell her straight. It's you and me from now on. It's what I wanted from the start."

Rachel smiled at the screen. "Can we meet up soon? Go for a drink and stuff?"

"Not yet."

He saw her pout and shake her head. It made her long blonde hair ripple in the sunshine pouring in through her bedroom window. He sighed. Blondes were his thing. He hadn't realised it before Megan. But now he had a type.

"My mum won't let me out after school anyway. The police have let that scumbag go. Everyone knows he killed Elsa."

"They'll have their reasons."

"He killed Elsa because she bullied Gaby. I don't think the police have realised that yet."

"Thick, the lot of them."

"Trouble is, all I've got on my laptop is a photo, and it could be of anyone. How do I know it's you?"

"It is me, Rachel. I look exactly like that photo. Elsa must have shown you the one she carried in her purse. It was taken when I was in a band at uni last year," he said.

"You were in a band?"

"Don't get too excited. We weren't very good."

"Can I tell people about you?"

"You can tell Megan." He watched her lie back and stretch out on the bed. "Tell her tomorrow. Once she knows, we can meet up."

He smiled to himself. There was no chance of that, not yet anyway. He only met them when their time was up. Now time was up for Megan, so he was ready to groom another one. He'd have the lovely Rachel waiting in the wings, eager to take her place.

He inhaled deeply. He would take Megan tomorrow on her way to school. He'd been patient. Megan was beautiful. By this time tomorrow that beauty would be gone. He'd have had his fun and Megan would be dead meat.

Rachel interrupted his reverie. "Why did you choose me?"

"Because you've got lovely tits." He watched her sit up. Her eyes dipped to her chest. She teased him, running her slim little fingers tantalisingly down the buttons on her shirt.

"Want to see them?"

"Good girl. I'd like that very much."

* * *

They sat in the parked car. Ruth stared ahead. "It was a hideous case and you got too close. You weren't in charge either, Reynolds was. Have you ever considered, Tom, that all that

61

blind anger, the need to get Donnelly at all costs, was fuelled by Reynolds? He had Kennet watching his every move. He was obsessed. It made him ill. He was never the same after that case. In the file it says that Donnelly made a complaint against Reynolds. Accused him of being on his back long before Annabelle Roper was killed."

Calladine looked her in the face. He was still angry. "I lived the case, remember? There was solid evidence and the jury found him guilty based on it. Plus there were other factors. Donnelly had no alibi for the time Annabelle was missing."

"All I'm saying is that we mustn't presume that Elsa Ramsden is down to Donnelly just because of the past. We have to look harder. There will be better forensic evidence this time. You cannot go near that man again unless it clearly points his way. You can't hound him, Tom. Birch and that scary vicar will have your job."

Calladine sighed. "Say we do cross Donnelly off the list for now. Who else is in the frame?"

"I've no idea, but we can start with Megan Heywood. We find out more about what those girls get up to, and who with. While we're at it, we look at that chat room they're all so fond of."

Was Ruth right? Calladine had worked with her for a long time and she was rarely wrong. But then again, she'd just come back after being out of the job for a while. She'd be rusty. A long weekend was enough to take the edge off him. He couldn't make up his mind. "What time is it?" he asked.

"Gone four. Megan will have left school by now. We could go round to her house."

"Okay."

"But softly does it. These girls are wary. And they can be good liars."

Calladine was surprised. "You don't suspect one of them, surely?"

"No, of course not. But Megan and the rest know more about Elsa's life than anyone. They are our way in, but we have to be careful not to frighten them into silence. They clam up and we'll be chasing our tails."

Calladine nodded. Ruth talked a lot of sense. "Who else was friends with Elsa?"

"According to Jake there are four of them. Elsa, Megan, a Rachel Hayes and Sophie Briggs. They keep themselves apart. The others in the class aren't that fond of them. All four are from the Hobfield. Jake reckons they intimidate some of the younger pupils. Nothing heavy, simple run-of-the-mill bullying — if there is such a thing!"

"Gaby Donnelly?"

"Not liked. She is different because her mother has money. She's an accountant with a few famous clients, and the two of them get invited to places. Gaby is the butt of umpteen practical jokes. Always has been, all through school."

"The photo being the latest. I'll speak to the headmaster. We need the kids to delete that image off their phones." Calladine nodded at the end house in a row of four. "Here we are. Megan lives here and Elsa was half a dozen further down there. You can see why they'd knock about together."

"Kid gloves. Megan will have known more about Elsa's life than anyone. That's what teenage girls are like. They share stuff with one another, not with family," Ruth reminded him.

"When did you become such an expert?"

"I was one once, remember?"

Calladine smiled. "Her mother's at the door. She doesn't look too happy."

Dawn Heywood was standing with her arms folded, watching them. "You had him, but now he's free again. What the hell's going on?"

"Had who, Mrs Heywood?" asked Ruth.

"It's *Miss*. That bastard Donnelly. We all know he killed Elsa, and we all know why. So what are you going to do about it?"

Ruth took a breath. "As yet we have no solid evidence, so there isn't much we can do."

Miss Heywood took a step backwards. "Bloody useless, the lot of you. I suppose you want to speak to our Megan. You'd better come in."

Word had travelled fast. They'd only spoken to Donnelly that afternoon. Calladine would love to know who was doing all the talking. "Is she okay?"

"What do you think? Her best mate got murdered. She was part of the lot that teased Gaby, so she thinks she's next."

"We can have her watched," Ruth suggested.

"God, no! We take care of our own round here."

Megan Heywood was on the stairs, listening.

Ruth smiled. "Hello again! We thought a chat might benefit us all, if you don't mind?"

She was still wearing her school uniform. The girl's long blonde hair was loose about her shoulders. Despite the make-up plastered all over her face, she looked younger than her eighteen years.

She began speaking straight away. "Elsa was worse than the rest of us. She wouldn't stop. She hated Gaby. Now I'm in the frame for texting that damn photo to my friends. My mum thinks he'll come after me next."

"Elsa's death might not have anything to do with all that," Ruth said.

"Course it does. Gaby told her dad. She was seen talking to him. He was waiting on her road. He's killed before."

"Come through. I'll make a pot of tea," Megan's mother said.

Ruth continued. "Did Elsa have a boyfriend? Perhaps someone she didn't tell her mum about."

"She was seeing Peachy, her brother's friend. But that cooled. He was a lot older than her, and I don't think Danny approved. Since him, I don't really know."

Calladine's ears pricked up at the sound of the nickname.

"Do you know why the relationship cooled?" asked Ruth.

Megan shook her head. "Like I said, he's older, and he's been in trouble with you lot."

"What sort of trouble?"

"Just a bit of dealing. He's not like that now though. He's made a fresh start."

Calladine shook his head. "You seem to know a lot about him. Do you like this bloke too, Megan?"

"When he's right, he's okay. He likes a good time and takes us round the clubs. I've been out with him, Danny and Megan a couple of times. Nothing serious."

"What do you mean — when he's right?" Ruth asked.

"He's not easy to keep tabs on. He always has someone or other after him. That's why I've not seen him recently. I think he's scared. Keeping his head down."

"Do you know who he's frightened of?"

"Danny Ramsden I think. They used to be friends but something happened. They fell out about something, could have been money."

"Can I have his full name?" asked Ruth.

"Why? Will he get in trouble? He's had nothing to do with Elsa or any of us for ages. This isn't down to him."

Ruth smiled. "We simply need to check him out, that's all."

Megan sighed. "Liam Peach."

Calladine had thought as much. He knew a man with the nickname Peachy. What he couldn't understand was why these girls would be interested in someone like him. Peachy was a small-time drug dealer on the Hobfield. Perhaps that was it. He was their supplier.

Calladine changed tack. "Tell us about this chat room you all use. How did you find out about it?"

"An email I think. I can't really remember. We all use it, the whole class. There are lots of different ones out there. But the one we use is very good. The guy who runs it is called Aiden. He answers questions about homework and stuff. He's really cool."

"Where does he live?"

"Exeter. Miles away."

"Is there anyone you know of who might want to do Elsa harm?" Calladine asked her.

"Half the school at some time or other. Elsa was tough. She didn't put up with no crap. Cross her and you got a pasting."

Calladine wondered if Jake Ireson knew about any of this. "How about outside school?"

"Her brother Danny got mixed up in something a few weeks back. Elsa was really worried about him. He owed money to someone. I know he asked Peachy to help him out, but he refused. Said he was broke himself. They kept arguing and it ended up with a fight."

"Do you know who Danny owed money to?" Calladine said.

Megan shook her head. "Elsa never said."

"You said Gaby was seen talking to her father. When was this?"

"When she got off the bus at lunchtime today. He was waiting for her. She wasn't happy about it, but they did speak for a few minutes. She could have told him anything — what we did, where we live. The man's a maniac."

Megan's mother interrupted. "She'll be fine. We'll look after her. If necessary, I'll keep her under lock and key until Donnelly's inside again."

Ruth gave each of them her card. "If you want to talk, Megan, or if anything occurs to you, then give me a ring. Doesn't matter when it is."

Megan Heywood gave Ruth a big smile. "Better not ring you at night. Mr Ireson won't like it!"

Ruth smiled back. "I think it'll be baby Ireson that'll grumble."

"Mr Ireson is really nice, we all like him. You're dead lucky, you are."

They left the house. Calladine said, "When we get back I'll be sure to check that notebook Donnelly left with us. See if he made any mention of meeting his daughter today."

"Whether it's there or not it makes no difference. It's not evidence that he hurt Elsa, Tom. Now — Gaby Donnelly? Or do we go and find Danny Ramsden?" Ruth said firmly.

"I think we should check out Danny and his friend Liam Peach before we go any further. I want to know why Peach is so interested in those girls. It might be better to bring them into the station for a chat," Calladine said.

"You recognised that name, didn't you? I saw the look on your face."

"Liam Peach is old enough to be the father of any one of those girls. And he used to be big pals with Donnelly."

Ruth stared at him. "What are you getting at?"

"I don't know yet. I need to think about it."

CHAPTER 8

"Sir, Shelley Mortimer rang in. She wants you to ring her back urgently."

They'd returned to the office. Calladine checked his mobile — nothing. Then he saw that the battery was dead. "Thanks, Joyce." He dialled Shez's number.

"Sorry, love, I need to charge the bloody thing. To be honest, I think I need a new one. I've had this one for years."

Shez ignored the small talk. "I need to see you, Tom. Today, as soon as you can get away."

She sounded upset. Her voice was shaky. Not like her at all. "Something bothering you?"

But Shez didn't explain. "The Wheatsheaf in an hour, and don't be late. Don't bring half the nick with you either. What I've got to say is delicate."

What now? Shez was a great girl, but her life was complicated. This latest problem could be anything. Calladine looked at Ruth. "You should get off. I'm going to prepare the briefing notes for the morning, then I'll have to go too."

"Got you under her thumb, has she?" Ruth said.

Calladine grinned. "She misses me. Can't say I blame her."

"Big-headed sod! See you in the morning."

Calladine retired to his office to try and make sense of what they'd got. No one wanted him on Donnelly's tail, so he'd have to play smart. And now another name had come up — Liam Peach. Calladine looked at the Annabelle Roper case notes and found that Peach got a mention. He and Donnelly had fought a couple of days before they found the body. When he'd been arrested, Donnelly had bruises all over his face. He maintained that was down to Peach. At the time Peach had admitted as much, but not the reason why they'd fought. Tomorrow Calladine would get Imogen to check what Peach had been up to recently. Another name caught his eye — one he'd forgotten. It was Dawn Heywood, Megan's mother. He could have kicked himself. She'd been seeing Donnelly at the time of the murder. She'd been asked for a statement about his whereabouts, but had refused to speak. Among the notes was one written by Reynolds. He'd circled the date of Annabelle's murder, and written the name Dawn Heywood and a question mark. Calladine had no idea what this meant, or what had been going on in the DI's mind at the time. But the way things were going, he might get the opportunity to ask him.

Then there was Danny Ramsden. Why was he going around with a no-mark like Peach? Drugs? And why had they argued? They'd be sure to ask him when he came in.

They still had a number of the sixth formers to speak to. Rachel Hayes and Sophie Griggs might know something Megan didn't. Then there was Gaby. He'd get Ruth to sort the girls, along with Rocco. She understood them better than he did.

Calladine flicked through the Elsa Ramsden case notes again. Donnelly was involved in this, he was sure of it. He intended to go through the notebook with a fine-tooth comb, check out every entry. He'd do it himself, quietly.

* * *

Shez's greeting was brusque. "I said an hour. I've got you a drink. Let's sit in the corner over there." She pointed to an empty table under an amplifier.

Calladine grimaced as they sat down. "Bit noisy."

Shez's response was, "I don't want anyone listening to what we're talking about."

"What's up?" He watched as she fiddled with her red polished nails, obviously nervous. Shez hadn't been in his life for long. She was nearly ten years younger than Calladine and was looking stunning. She had black, chin-length hair, wide cheekbones and a full mouth, always bright with her signature red lippy. He was always half expecting her to come to her senses and dump him. He couldn't quite believe she wanted to be with him.

Now Shez's bottom lip was quivering. "Something's happened. I'm only telling you, Tom, because I need your help. Your *unofficial* help. It was made quite clear that I shouldn't go near the police."

Calladine's heart sank. "Depends what it is. Just spit it out and then we'll see."

"One of my girls has gone missing."

This had happened before, so why the big deal? Shez ran a model and escort agency. The girls often accompanied wealthy clients and sometimes that meant impromptu weekends away. "Why so upset? She'll come back."

"No, I don't think she will. Not unless we intervene." Shez passed him an envelope. "Read the letter inside."

The note was brief. It was a ransom demand. Kate Reynolds had been kidnapped. Two hundred thousand pounds was being demanded for her release. Calladine looked up at Shez. "Is this genuine? Are you sure it's not some scam, or a joke?"

Shez shook her head. "That's what I thought at first. But look inside the envelope again."

Calladine peered inside and found a lock of dark brown hair tied up with pink ribbon.

"It's Kate's hair. The last sentence states that if I don't pay, he'll send her back to me, piece by piece."

Calladine took a long swig of his beer and leaned back in his seat. "This can't stay unofficial, Shez. Kate is in danger. I have to give this letter and its contents to our forensic people. You have to formally report this."

"They'll kill her. It says so there." A red nail tapped at the threatening sentence. "I can't risk her life! I'd never forgive myself. I'm begging you, Tom. Do something! Find Kate for me. Catch the bastard who took her."

"When did you get this?"

"This morning. It must have been shoved through the door of my flat. There is no stamp or postmark."

"Did anyone see anything? You live above your office. You have a girl manning the phones all day."

"The flat has its own entrance, round the back. No one saw, and there are no cameras round there either."

"Has Kate — or you — upset anyone recently?"

She sighed. "No more than usual, Tom. You know my business is fraught with possibilities. My clients in the escort side can get a bit tricky at times. But Kate hasn't done any escort work. She's a model, and she just gets on with the job. She's been doing a shoot for a high-street shop, modelling their winter range."

"Have you heard anything from the kidnapper since the note?"

"I had a call on the office phone at lunchtime. It was a man. He said he'd be in touch with his instructions within the next twenty-four hours. If I don't do as he wants, he'll harm Kate."

"The call . . ."

"I dialled 1471 the minute he rang off, but the number was withheld."

"We have to report this," Calladine said firmly.

Shez didn't reply. Her hand shook as she reached for her drink.

"It will be a low-key investigation. Whoever has taken Kate won't even realise," Calladine said.

"You can't promise that. Will you lead the investigation, Tom?"

He knew that was unlikely. "I can't. I'm involved, and I'm currently investigating a murder."

"So who will they put in charge? Kate lives in Leesdon, with her father."

With her father? Calladine looked at her. "Any relation to Alan Reynolds?"

"He's her dad, he's ex-police."

A name from the past. Calladine's old boss in fact.

"Yes, I've worked with him. Rest assured that whoever takes the case will do a good job. My colleagues know what they are doing."

Calladine went through the options. The other team at the nick were headed up by DI Brad Long, who was on annual leave. That left DS Don Thorpe, which gave him no confidence at all. He couldn't say that to Shez.

* * *

Jake Ireson sat on the sofa, cuddling his son. "It's been a bloody awful day. After the visit from you two, the group just wouldn't settle. I had a meeting with the head so I had no choice but to leave them with Robert. They're a heartless bunch when they spot weakness. They home in — and twist the knife."

Ordinarily, Ruth didn't have much time to spare for Leesdon Comp's sad new recruit, but it did have a bearing on the case. "What's wrong with him?"

"He can't hack it. God knows I've tried, both with him and the kids. But they take every opportunity to make mincemeat of him. Unless he learns how to handle teenagers he'll have to call it a day. His nerves won't stand the strain."

"Has he spoken to you?"

"That's a big part of the problem. Robert won't admit that he's got a problem. I left him for twenty minutes this afternoon, and when I got back the kids had gone berserk. They were throwing stuff around the room, someone was playing music from their phone, and four or five of them were even dancing! Robert was virtually cowering at his desk. The kids quietened down the second they spotted me, but I know what I saw, and so does Robert."

"You can't sort him on your own. Tell the head or whoever deals with problems of that sort. Surely he's had training? Why go into teaching if you can't cope with kids?"

Jake handed Harry to her. "Here's one kid that knows what he wants — his mum. Amy at the nursery said he's had a lovely time today. He's been digging in the sandpit and watching some of the bigger kids play football."

"Football?"

"Some bloke comes in once a week and teaches them. Girls and boys, and in all weathers. 'Football Freddie,' they call him."

"He's going to love that when he gets older."

"How was your first day back?"

Ruth shrugged. "Oh, you know. One murder, a killer newly released from Strangeways and Calladine playing maverick again. Apart from that, easy!"

"The head got a call before we finished this afternoon. We know about Elsa, but we haven't told the kids yet."

"Doesn't matter. They'll all know by now. Megan Heywood will see to that, I would imagine. She's convinced it's down to Gaby's father, Craig Donnelly. He's the newly released by the way. Calladine is convinced too. But I'm not so sure."

"Elsa was a dark horse, Ruth. She might have been still a schoolkid, but she had some dodgy friends. Not the least of them being Liam Peach. He's a long-time drug dealer off the Hobfield, when he's not inside. They had some sort of romance going on a few months ago. And I cannot begin to understand what she saw in him. When I heard I put it down to drugs, and he had plenty of money."

Ruth shook her head. "Well, he hasn't now, according to the latest tittle-tattle."

"Around that time there was a rumour that Elsa had got herself pregnant, and had an abortion. But check that before you use it."

Ruth kissed him. "And there was me thinking you didn't pick up on things. Well done! We'll make a detective of you yet."

"No thanks. I'm happy where I am."

CHAPTER 9

Wednesday

"While some of you were having a life last night, I was sat in here preparing this report of where we're at." Calladine passed around several sheets of paper to his team of three. "Rocco and Imogen, I want you to find Liam Peach and bring him in for a chat. Try the local bookies. That's his favourite haunt of late. While you're doing that I'll get a couple of uniform to bring in Danny Ramsden. Keep them apart. I don't want them coordinating on their stories. Ruth, would you return to Leesdon Comp and speak to Rachel and Sophie? Get them on their own. See if they say anything different from yesterday. Remember how Rachel came back and gave us that little titbit. This afternoon we'll both go and see Gaby Donnelly and her mother."

"It might be worth having a private chat with Robert Clarke while I'm there. He's the NQT who's working with Jake. He's not coping. Those girls are making his life hell. Just a thought," added Ruth.

"If you think it'll get us anywhere. It's a big leap from suffering a bit of flak to killing one of your pupils."

"I'm not suggesting that. But he may know things. They tease him, say stuff out of turn."

Calladine turned to Joyce. "Would you arrange the meeting with the Donnellys? I don't mind where, either the school or their home."

A uniformed officer stuck his head around the door. "Sir, your visitor is downstairs."

Calladine smiled. "Would you show her into the soft interview room, please, Jack? Right folks, get to it. We'll meet back here at lunchtime and see what we've got."

Ruth began putting her stuff together. "Who's visiting you?"

Calladine pulled a face. "Shez."

"Why, what's she done? And why the face?"

"I'll tell you later. It's sensitive. Actually it's worse than that, it's damned tricky. I'm not sure how it's going to go, either."

"A problem with Shez, eh? Is that because you stayed late last night to do your homework? Throw a strop in the Wheatsheaf, did she?"

"It's nothing like that. She needs my help. She had something to tell me. After that neither of us was in the mood for small talk, so I came back. This case won't crack itself, Ruth. Plus, given what Shez told me, we might have something else on our hands very soon."

"More work? What's wrong with Long's team taking up the slack?"

"He's on holiday, so that leaves Thorpe. Shez needs help, not some joker who'll just sit around ogling her girls."

Ruth was curious now. "Come on then. What's it about?"

"I can't discuss it yet." He saw her face — Ruth was going to do her best to wheedle it out of him. "I'll tell you later, I promise. Let me have the meeting first."

Ruth wagged her finger at him. "You're being cagey, Calladine. What happened to that partnership you were so big on yesterday?"

He was saved by the office phone ringing.

It was Rhona Birch, and she was not pleased. "We're waiting, Inspector."

"On my way, ma'am."

Ruth grinned. "Go on then, get to it. Birch doesn't appreciate being kept hanging around."

* * *

"According to the boss, he hangs out in the bookies." Rocco checked his watch. "Will they be open this time of the morning?"

"We'll park up and wait. By the time we get him back, uniform should have collected Danny Ramsden off the Hobfield."

Rocco was reading through Calladine's report. "Liam Peach knows Donnelly. He's about the same age too, they're both in their late forties. So what's he doing, going out with young girls?"

"Some blokes are like that. Some girls prefer older men too."

"Weird if you ask me."

Imogen edged into a space a few yards away from the bookies. The shops were just opening and there were plenty of folk about already. "We have no address for Peach. The last one was his mother's, but uniform said he left there months ago. If we don't catch him here we've got a search on our hands."

Rocco pointed to a bloke standing outside the bookies' door. "Well, we're in luck. That's him. Let's go."

Imogen showed the man her badge. "Liam Peach? DCs Rockliffe and Goode, Leesdon CID. We'd like you to come down to the station for a little chat."

Peach sounded annoyed. "Bugger off! I've got a business to run. The punters will be along shortly. Don't want to disappoint them, do we?"

Imogen pointed to the sign painted across the window. "You own this place? It says *Johnson's*."

Peach gave her an oily smile. "Got himself into a bit of a mess, did Jonny. So I helped him out, and we did a deal. This place belongs to me now."

"You've done well. Jonny's been here for years. It must have been some mess," Rocco said.

"Nice try, copper, but I'm not saying 'owt. What went on between Jonny and me is private."

Liam Peach was looking smarter than he had in years. He wore a sharp suit, his hair was neat. The car parked outside the bookies was new too. Imogen was impressed by the turnaround. It wasn't so long ago that he was rumoured to be living rough.

"Where are you living?" she asked.

Peach coughed, dug a packet of cigarettes out of his pocket and lit one. "None of your bloody business. I need to get this place open. What d'you want?"

Rocco came back with, "Craig Donnelly. Have you seen him since he got out?"

Peach paled visibly. "That waste of space. No. Better things to do." He nodded at the shop.

"You used to be friends. I would have thought he'd have looked you up," Rocco continued.

Peach's eyes darted up and down the street. "Once maybe, but not now."

"Had a fall out?"

"He's done time. He's a killer. I run a respectable business now. I don't want my name tarnished by the likes of him. This is a new start for me."

He had spoken with conviction. Imogen nodded. "Come with us. A quick chat and we'll bring you back. A couple of hours, tops."

A young woman arrived. "Mr Peach, what's going on?"

Peach handed her a set of keys and smiled at her. "Nothing, Alison. Open up and hold the fort until I get back. These people want me to help them with something."

The girl smiled and opened the shop door. Imogen noted that she was young. No more than twenty. Liam Peach evidently still had a thing for young girls.

"Do you know Elsa Ramsden or Megan Heywood?" Imogen asked.

"Yeah, stupid slags the pair of them. What've they been up to now? Is that what this is all about? Dragged my name into something, have they?"

Rocco gestured towards their car. "Our car is over there, Liam. A quick chat, nothing heavy. We might even manage some breakfast."

Liam Peach chucked the fag end into the gutter and followed them to the car.

They drove back in silence.

Joyce looked up when they entered the incident room. "Ramsden is in room seven."

"Good. We've put Peach in twelve. We'll speak to Ramsden first. Peachy's having breakfast. Boss in?"

"He's downstairs with Birch. Don't know what's going on, but he wasn't telling Ruth anything."

"We'll wait until he gets back before we start the interviews."

* * *

DS Don Thorpe was speaking to Shez Mortimer. "When was the last time you saw Miss Reynolds?"

Calladine, Birch, Thorpe and Shez were in one of the soft interview rooms. Calladine was pleased to see that Thorpe had a pen handy and, for once, was taking notes.

"I saw her Friday lunchtime. She'd finished a photo shoot and was off home for the weekend."

"Did she arrive home?" asked Birch.

"No. I checked with her dad. He didn't get unduly worried over the weekend. He presumed that Kate was working. I rang him this morning when I got the note."

"Kate lives in Leesdon," Calladine told Thorpe. "Her dad used to work here. He was my DI before he retired and I got made up to inspector."

Thorpe noted it down, and grinned. "I'll have to watch myself in that case. Does she drive home?"

Shez shook her head. "Kate took the train. My office is on the outskirts of Manchester — Droylsden."

"So we don't know where she disappeared," Birch added.

"We do," said Shez. "Kate rang me from Leesdon station. She'd left her make-up bag in the office and she asked me to keep it safe for her."

Calladine frowned. "So, somewhere between the railway station and her home. Where exactly does she live, Shez?"

"Her dad lives in one of those cottages down by the canal, Tom." Shez wrote down the address for Thorpe.

"And no one else has rung you during these last few days, asking about her?" Birch said.

Shez turned to her. "No. She has no boyfriend, there's just her dad. When I got the note I rang him and said that she'd gone away for a few days on a job. I didn't want to worry him. This is his phone number."

"The kidnapper is using your office phone. We'll put a tap on it. We'll record all calls from now on," said Birch.

Calladine was puzzled. "Why not ask her dad for the money? It would make more sense."

Shez shrugged. "I've no idea. Perhaps he imagines I'm good for it. But there is no way I can find that amount of money." Shez turned to Birch. "What happens when I get instructions for dropping it off? He'll know straight away."

"Let us worry about that," said Birch.

"This is a recent photo of Kate." Shez handed Thorpe a photo of a young woman with dark shoulder length hair and deep blue eyes.

"Have you been aware of anyone hanging around recently? Paying any unusual attention to Kate?" Thorpe asked.

"Nothing obvious. We all simply get on with the job. The girls go to the various shoots in taxis and we keep in touch by mobile."

Birch spoke with certainty. "This will be someone who has been watching you. You may even know him. The kidnapper knows how you work, and what buttons to press to get the results he wants. Hard as it is, you have to keep it together. When he rings you, which he will, I want you to keep him talking for as long as you can. This is vital if we're to trace him.

Do anything you have to. Play the upset female card. Beg him to let her go. Promise him anything, whatever it takes to keep him on the line. We will be listening and doing our best to discover where he's calling from."

"If he's watching me, he'll know I've come here today. He'll know I've spoken to you. I could be signing Kate's death warrant right now!"

"If he's done his homework, he'll know about your relationship with Calladine. The two of you will leave together. Appear happy, laugh a little," Birch said.

"That is a point, ma'am. He is taking a risk with the *no police* thing. *If* he does know about me and Shez."

"Could be he's rubbing our noses in it. Getting his hands on the money might only be part of what he's after."

Calladine hadn't considered that. Birch was a shrewd one.

"Our people will be at your office within the hour. No one need know what they're up to. As far as anyone is concerned, you have a network problem and they are IT technicians come to fix it."

Shez looked at Calladine. "Will it work? I have to get Kate back. I'll never forgive myself if anything happens to her."

Birch was firm. "We'll get her back. All you have to do, Miss Mortimer, is exactly what you're told. No heroics, no taking off on your own with the inspector here. You keep DS Thorpe up to speed with every event. Any contact with the kidnapper at all, you let us know."

Calladine took Shez's hand. "He may phone, but he might also leave you another note. Or even send an email. Despite all our preparations, contact won't necessarily be by phone."

Thorpe picked up the evidence bag containing the envelope. "The hair. We should have it tested. Make sure it does belong to Kate."

Birch nodded. "Arrange what you need with the Duggan."

"I'll get you something of Kate's to match the DNA with. Will a toothbrush do?"

Thorpe nodded.

Shez was still looking at Calladine. "I'm scared. Nothing like this has ever happened before. This monster could do anything to Kate. You have to find her! Bring her back."

"Could you or someone else who works in your business have upset anyone? Kate's kidnap may have been opportunist, you see. It could be that any one of you would have done. He could be getting revenge for something," Thorpe asked.

Shez gave a small smile. "In the course of an average week I upset no end of people, Sergeant. It comes with the job. Particularly the escort side of it. Some of my customers can be reluctant to pay. Or they can be very demanding. Usually it works out fine. Off the top of my head, I can't think of anyone I've upset so much that they'd resort to kidnap!"

Birch got to her feet. "We'll get started. Thorpe — background on the missing girl. With the best will in the world, Miss Mortimer will not know everything that's going on in Kate Reynolds's life. And keep me posted."

Thorpe nodded. "I'll get the technical people organised. You two go play nice, but don't draw attention to yourselves. There's nothing wrong — remember?"

* * *

Jake Ireson stood with Ruth in his office. "Do you want to speak to them both together or one at a time?"

"One at a time, I think. They won't be so guarded. I'll see Rachel first."

"Is that okay? Don't you need an adult present?"

"They are both eighteen, Jake. Do they know about Elsa now?"

"Yes, I had a word with them this morning. They've been as quiet as mice since. Most of them found out last night. No doubt Megan told them. She hasn't come in today."

"That's understandable. She'll be upset."

"I'll go and sort the girls. I can't stay, I'm afraid. Robert hasn't turned up either, so I'm covering his class this afternoon. And not a word, not so much as a phone call or text."

"Thrown in the towel, has he?"

Jake shook his head. "He needs to get a grip."

Jake disappeared, returning moments later with Rachel Hayes.

Ruth smiled at her. "Sorry to drag you away. Given what's happened, I'm after some background on Elsa. You know the sort of thing — boyfriends, particularly those she kept secret from her brothers. We all know that teenage girls have secrets. That's normal. But this is no time to hold back. We have to find who killed Elsa."

Rachel's face fell. "She didn't have anyone. At least, not at the moment."

"So who was her last boyfriend?"

Rachel gazed at the floor. "I'm not sure."

"Did she go out with Liam Peach?"

Rachel nodded. "But it wasn't what everyone thought. Peachy was soft on her, so she used him, took him for a mug. He sold her drugs — practically gave them to her. Elsa passed the stuff on to her brother Danny and he sold it on. They made a packet. But then Peachy got wind of what was going on and cut Elsa out. He was really angry. Said he'd fix Danny for doing him out of his share."

"Was Peachy angry with Elsa?"

"Yes. At first he was raging, but then he and Danny struck up some sort of deal and everything settled down."

"Has anyone else been hanging round? Making a nuisance of themselves with Elsa?"

Rachel shook her head.

Ruth persisted. "She was a pretty girl. I can't believe she didn't have a boyfriend."

Rachel's cheeks were reddening. "Perhaps she did. But he wasn't anyone local. She's never actually met up with him. None of us have. Not even Megan. It's an online thing."

Warning bells were ringing in Ruth's head. "What do you mean, Rachel? Who are you talking about?"

"Aiden. The guy who runs the chat room. We all like him. But at first he was only interested in Elsa."

"At first?"

"They fell out after a few weeks. She didn't visit the chat room after that. Then he moved onto Megan. He told her she was special and that he liked her better. He likes blondes with long hair." Rachel was really blushing now.

Ruth looked at her. "Girls like you and Megan?"

"Megan reckons she'll be going down to Exeter during the next holidays, to see him."

"So Aiden was using the chat room as a sort of dating site? He went after you one at a time?"

Rachel shrugged. "Yes, you could put it like that."

Ruth was amazed that the girl saw nothing wrong in that. "What about helping with your coursework?"

"That was a sort of cover. If you weren't one of his special girls, he wasn't interested. So the others kept away."

"He didn't help with schoolwork, then?"

"No, not really. To be honest, I don't think he's even done his A levels. But in the beginning we all thought that's what we were joining. We didn't see any harm. Nothing could happen. It was just banter, flirting. You see, he lives too far away."

Surely the girl wasn't that naive? "I must insist that you and your friends give the chat room, or whatever it is, a rest until we've checked it out. Alright, Rachel?"

CHAPTER 10

Back from Leesdon Comp, Ruth Bayliss went in search of Calladine. "I think we could have a problem, guv. Speaking to Rachel Hayes on her own paid dividends. She told me that Liam Peach supplied drugs to Elsa, which in turn she passed onto her brother, Danny. Peachy liked her, so he gave her what she wanted. When he found out Danny was selling it on for a tidy profit, he got angry. Wanted his share."

"Sounds about right. What you're saying is that Elsa used him."

"Too right she did. If Peachy was that bothered, she must have been making a packet. *And* — that chat room is not so innocent either. In fact it's not even a chat room. Elsa and the others used that as a cover. They were actually talking online to a bloke called Aiden. He did the rounds, kept each of the girls dangling. When he dumped Elsa, he moved onto Megan. Now he's making a move on Rachel. She doesn't see the harm. She believes what he tells her, that he lives miles away in Exeter. Whereas we know he could be just down the road. Megan kept that little nugget quiet when we spoke to her."

Calladine groaned. "The day just gets better! Don't they realise the danger? This person they're talking to could be anyone. He could be the nutter we're looking for!"

"I would have spoken to Megan but she's not in school today. Robert Clarke isn't in either, and he didn't ring in sick or anything. Jake puts it down to the way the kids have been behaving with him. Reckons he's done a runner."

"Ring Megan's mother. See how she is. If the girl is up to it, we need to talk to her about this bloody Aiden. How about the other girl, Sophie Griggs?"

Ruth was already picking up the phone. "She's had no part in it. She has dark hair. Apparently this freak, Aiden, likes them blonde."

Rocco called over, "Your office phone is ringing, guv."

Calladine listened to the familiar voice. "Julian! What have you got for us?"

"I'm working on the Elsa Ramsden case with Doctor Barrington. I've done some initial work on Elsa's burnt hand. The method used is very different to what was done to Annabelle Roper. If you remember, Donnelly dunked her right hand into a pan of boiling chip fat. Not so with Elsa. Whoever did it soaked a cloth in petrol, wrapped it around Elsa's hand, then set it alight."

Yet another difference to add to Ruth's list. "Copycat? Someone who got hold of half the story and is trying to make it look like Donnelly is to blame?"

"I can't say, Tom. I just look after the science."

"Anything else?"

"Not yet. Some of the tests are taking longer. Worth doing, though. The girl had allergic reactions to all sorts of stuff. The glue on the tape used to bind her limbs, for example. The inside of her throat, nose and lungs was inflamed from something she inhaled. That happens when a person suffers with hay fever. I would say it was a violent reaction that would have come on quick. I'm trying to identify the trigger. It might lead us somewhere."

"Thanks, Julian. I'll speak to her mother about that."

Ruth called him as he walked back into the incident room. She looked worried. "Problem. Megan's mum says she went to school this morning. My phone call has got her terrified. She didn't want to let Megan out of her sight, but says that she must have sneaked out when she left for work. When her mum got home after lunch she presumed Megan had gone to school."

"Ring round, see if she's at one of her friends' places."

"Unlikely. I've just come from school, remember? They're all there."

"In that case, we need to speak to Rachel Hayes again. Imogen, contact the school. Ask them to get hold of Rachel's mother. Arrange for a car to bring them both in."

Ruth frowned. "I don't think Rachel was holding back. She told me about the drugs. And she was very candid about the so-called chat room and the lad who runs it."

"Another little talk won't hurt. Where are IT with Elsa's laptop?"

Imogen told him. "We passed it over to the Duggan, sir. The guy who's having a look is Matt Hewson. He's good. If there's anything to find, then he's the one to do it."

"Get him on the phone. We need an update urgently."

"Danny Ramsden and Liam Peach are still waiting downstairs, sir," Rocco reminded Calladine.

"Okay. Ruth, you and Rocco take Ramsden and Imogen and I will talk to Peach."

Calladine waited while Imogen finished the phone calls.

"Mrs Hayes has picked Rachel up already. They've gone to a university open day in Manchester, so it will have to be tomorrow, guv. Matt is emailing an interim report. But it was definitely not a bona fide chat room the girls were visiting. For starters, it was located on the dark web."

* * *

Liam Peach was looking impatient. "You lot must think I've nothing better to do. Any more tea going? I'm parched sitting here."

Calladine nodded at the uniform, who went off to get him another mug.

Calladine quickly read through the notes Imogen had made. "You've come up in the world. Taken over the bookies, I see. Turned your life around, Peachy. Tell me how it happened. Where did you get the money from for a start?"

"Jonny had problems, debt mostly. He was about to ditch the place and run. I stepped in and got the whole lot for a song."

"Lucky you. That business is pretty established. You should do well."

Peach leaned back in his chair. "Wish folk would leave me alone to get on with it."

"Why did you fall out with Danny Ramsden?"

Peach pulled a face. "That sister of his wants her lights punching out. Stupid bitch dropped me right in it."

"Elsa? What did she do?"

"She used me. Really stitched me up. Got me to get stuff for her, didn't she?"

"That stuff being drugs."

"Look, copper, I didn't come here to get banged up for dealing. It wasn't like that. It was just a bit of blow for personal use."

"For now, let's say I believe that little fairy tale. Did Danny object?"

"No — the reverse. He wanted me to get more. Said he'd do me over if I refused. But I couldn't get anything. I've been out of circulation for a while so I don't know the right people anymore. He was having none of it. We had a bit of a scrap outside the pub one night. I gave him a wide berth for a while and it fizzled out. We're okay now."

"When did you last see Elsa?"

"A couple of weeks ago. She was being a pain. Despite what had happened, she kept on at me to get her more drugs."

"Did you tell Danny?"

"No, I'm keeping well away. If he tries it on again I'll be complaining to you lot."

"I don't think he will. He's got other things on his mind at the moment."

Peachy looked from one officer to the other. "I heard something about Elsa. Is it true?"

"I'm afraid it is."

"That's got nothing to do with me. I haven't seen the slag in ages. I told you."

"Seen anything of Craig Donnelly since he got out?"

Peach's eyes shot up to meet Calladine's. He'd struck a nerve. "Why would I want to see him?"

"You tell me. But you and him do have history, you can't deny that. You beat him up quite badly just before he got arrested for the Annabelle Roper killing. The bloke was covered in bruises."

Liam Peach was squirming now. "Nothing was ever proved. You can't pin that on me."

Calladine ignored this. "Why did you do it? Did you know what he'd done?"

"I'd no idea that girl was down to him."

Calladine didn't pause. "Did you know Annabelle Roper?"

"What makes you ask that?"

"Just answer the question. Did you know her?"

"Everyone on the estate knew her. She was alright really. Shame what happened. I didn't know Donnelly had done it. And I didn't beat him up."

"Yes, you did. You admitted as much at the time. So why say you didn't?"

"Can I go now? This isn't official. That other copper said it was just a chat."

"Questions getting too tricky for you?"

Peach folded his arms. "Bloody coppers! Go and drag some other poor bugger in here and wind him up. I've had enough! And I've got a business to run."

They weren't going to get any more out of him. "We'll need an address," Imogen told him.

"I'm living in the flat above the bookies."

Calladine gestured to the uniform to escort Liam Peach out.

* * *

Back in the incident room, Rocco reported on the second interview. "Danny Ramsden insists he isn't after Peach, sir. Ten minutes tops, that's all we spent on him."

Ruth confirmed this. "Everything he said rang true. He was mystified when I suggested he was after Peach. He agreed there had been some bother a while ago. But given what has happened, Peach is way down Ramsden's list of priorities. He is really cut up about Elsa. He identified the body, said they were the worst moments of his life. He was very open about everything."

"So why did the girls think Peach was so scared, Ruth?"

Imogen chipped in. "Because of something else? It might be the drugs. He could be dealing to the kids on the quiet. He might even have still been supplying Elsa. But we'll never know that."

Calladine shook his head. "If you ask me, he was more scared of Donnelly."

"So why didn't he tell us, guv?" Imogen asked. "Come clean? Surely he must realise he'd be safer with us on side."

Calladine was unconvinced. "Because it's Liam Peach we're dealing with, a drug-dealing scally with a dodgy past and friends he wouldn't want us to know about."

Imogen was already tapping away on her keyboard. "I've got that report on the findings from Elsa's laptop, sir."

Calladine sighed. Imogen had said the chat room was on the dark web. In that case, what was the betting they'd got very little?

"The site works a bit like Skype, except that all the conversations are deleted once they're over. We know he spoke to Elsa every day and always at the same time — early morning. The history records that much, but there's no web address. The one Megan gave Ruth was bogus. I think he probably contacts them, tells them to be online so he can access their computers."

Ruth was thinking aloud. "Early morning . . . Someone with somewhere to go. A job?"

"Or a time when the girls are bound to be in. Probably in their bedrooms getting ready for school," Imogen added.

"This Aiden didn't always initiate contact. The kids could contact the chat room during the day too, so how did that work?" Calladine reminded them.

Imogen was looking at her screen. "It didn't. When the meetings were unscheduled, the kids were directed to a genuine website. Matt says that unless that website recognised your IP address, you weren't allowed on."

Calladine peered over her shoulder. "Can we get anywhere with that?"

"Matt says it's been taken down. He's trying to find out who hosted it, but is having no luck. It could have been located on a server anywhere in the world."

"No chat room then. This Aiden, or whatever he's really called, is grooming the girls. He could have had Elsa, Megan and God knows who else on the go at the same time. The girls simply told anyone who got curious that they were talking about homework."

Imogen nodded. "That's about the size of it, sir. Matt is still working on it. He could come up with more. We'll have to give him time."

Calladine was grim. "Megan might not have time. Do we know the route she takes to school?"

"Up until this week she's walked with Elsa. Now she makes her own way. Meets up with the others on the High Street," Imogen said.

Calladine shouted across the room. "Rocco! Check every minute of CCTV you can find. We need to know if Megan made it to the High Street or not."

Rocco nodded. "There's a camera at the edge of the common too, sir."

"Good. At least if we can pin down a location and time, we might be able to work out where and when she went missing."

CHAPTER 11

"Where . . . where am I?"

The girl's plaintive cry cut into the dark silence of the empty room. She shouted out again. But there was no reply. Megan Heywood tried to move but it was impossible. She'd been bound to a chair. Still dressed in her school uniform, minus her coat, she was shivering with cold.

"Is anyone there? Please say something. How did I get here? I have to go home."

"You're with me, Megan."

The voice was coming from a distance. Megan squinted into the gloom. She was sure there was no one else here. Then she made out a flashing red light. A camera. He was using it to watch her. The realisation made her angry. Who did he think he was to do this to her? And how had he got her here? She struggled with the hazy memory of the day. The more she tried to remember, the more her head ached. Sudden panic made her feel sick. This must be what he'd done to her friend. That thought sent a shiver of ice down her spine. "Was it you who took Elsa?"

He laughed.

Megan had no idea what time of day it was. Her mother would be frantic. "You have to let me go! You've made a mistake.

I'm not like her. I didn't agree with what she did to Gaby. Please . . . you have to listen." She was pleading with the darkness.

The voice came back, "I expected gratitude. You've wanted this for long enough."

"Do I know you?" She was puzzled. Who did she know who'd do something like this?

"I won't keep you waiting much longer, Megan. I've been looking forward to this, counting down the days. I bet you never realised you were having such an effect on me, did you?"

She was shaking with fear. This guy was a nutcase, whoever he was. "You're sick! You won't get away with this."

She screamed and pulled hard against what bound her, but Megan was losing the battle. She turned to one side and vomited. It made her even thirstier.

"I know what you did to Elsa, but there is no need to harm me. Let me go and I won't say a word."

He chuckled. "That would be no fun at all, Megan. Anyway, it's too late. You are here now and you know too much."

She screamed again into the blackness of the room. The only response was his laughter.

"No one will hear you. No one will come. Try to calm yourself. I will soon put you out of your misery."

"You can't hurt me! The police will find out like they did with Elsa. You'll be caught and punished."

"I'll take my chances, Megan. No one is going to find you until it's too late."

He laughed again.

"You're mad!"

"You young girls make it too easy. You deserve everything you get."

"What are you going to do to me?" Her breath caught in her throat. She swallowed, dreading his reply.

"I'm going to kill you, Megan. Eventually. But first we're going to have some fun."

* * *

Calladine sat down next to Rocco. "Megan's walk to school?"

Rocco pointed at the screen. "I've spotted something, sir. This character follows her from the common to Byron's Lane, the small passageway that links Park Road with the High Street. I've looked further on but Megan doesn't appear again." He tapped the monitor. "She went missing here, I'll lay odds on it."

"Byron's Lane? It's only a few yards long, and narrow. You couldn't drive a car through there. Check with the school and with her mother. If no one knows where Megan is, I want a full forensic team in that alley. Get uniform to tape it off in the meantime, and arrange a house to house. Give me another look at the bloke who followed her."

The man was wearing a long coat. He walked hunched over. He had long untidy hair and a full beard. Calladine had seen him somewhere before. "Print that out for me," he told Rocco.

With the image in his hand, Calladine walked along the corridor to the other team's office. Calladine put the printout in front of DS Don Thorpe. "Birch asked you for some background on this bloke, Jason Kent. Did you get anything?"

"No. He's a ghost. There are plenty of Jason Kents out there, but none of them are him." Thorpe tapped the photo. "Look at him. All that facial hair — it's a disguise, and he's wearing a wig."

"So he could be anyone?"

"Got it in one. I've checked the prison CCTV. His age is difficult to guess from the way he walks. And I think the weight he appears to be carrying around his middle is padding."

"He'll have been searched, surely?"

Thorpe shrugged. "He could still get away with it. Plenty of clothing on top."

That meant if they wanted to know what he was doing visiting a murderer, they'd have to ask Donnelly himself. The Reverend Livings would not like that.

"You got nothing else? Just that he doesn't exist?" Calladine shook his head.

"That's about it. Can't waste any more time on it." Thorpe tapped another file.

"How is the Kate Reynolds case going?"

"Got her on CCTV too, at Leesdon station like your lady said. Shez is a real looker by the way. Don't know how you did it, but, respect!"

"The case, Thorpe! Keep your head on the case. That girl's life depends on it. We need her found."

Calladine left him to it. It would be a miracle if Thorpe found Kate. They needed more information.

On his return to the incident room, Calladine collared the DC. "Rocco? Do me a favour, but keep it quiet. Take this photo and see if anyone at Leesdon railway station remembers this woman. She got off the Manchester train late Friday lunchtime. I could do with knowing if she spoke to anyone, whether anyone met her and what she did when she left. Did she get a taxi or walk, for instance?"

"Does this have anything to do with Elsa or Megan, sir?"

"No. But this young woman is missing too. Don't make a meal of it, and keep all your enquiries low-key."

Rocco didn't look happy. "I was going to carry on with the CCTV on the High Street, sir."

"Have you spoken to Megan's mum?"

"She has no idea where she is. Apparently her mobile is switched off and that never happens."

"Ruth, do we know who Megan's service provider is?"

"I'll ask her mum."

"See if they can tell us when and where the phone was switched off. I'm going to declare Megan Heywood officially missing. I'll arrange for someone to go to the house. They can pick up her laptop while they're at it."

As Rocco left the office, Ruth looked up from her desk. "That's a different case you sent Rocco out on, isn't it?"

"Yes. One of Shez's girls is missing. Interestingly it's Kate Reynolds, daughter of my old DI. I don't know what that means, if anything. They've sent a ransom demand to Shez, but keep it to yourself. Thorpe is supposed to be handling it but he's getting nowhere."

"Why ask Shez for money? Why not Kate's father?"

"That's bothering me too. The truth is, we don't know that he hasn't. It could be that he's simply not reported it."

"Has Thorpe spoken to Reynolds?"

"I doubt it."

Ruth shook her head. "So that means you're going to. You're getting too involved. And now you've sent Rocco out on the other team's case. Birch won't like it."

"Birch won't find out."

Ruth sighed. "Back to what we're supposed to be doing, I've been on to Elsa's GP. Rachel Hayes said she might have been pregnant. The doctor wouldn't talk over the phone but he will see me if I go in. He rattled on about patient confidentiality until I told him what had happened. Now he's willing to talk candidly."

"Good work." Calladine looked at the office clock. "Why don't you get off? Call in at the surgery on your way home."

"Not a bad idea. Jake will be late. No Robert Clarke means he's got a lot on his plate. I can pick up Harry, take him home and give him his tea."

With the rest of the team out of the way, Calladine took another look at the CCTV of Leesdon High Street. No sign of Megan. He backtracked, picking her up crossing the edge of the common onto Park Road and approaching Byron's Lane. Jason Kent came into view behind her. He followed until they both disappeared into the lane.

Jason Kent, whoever he really was, had visited Donnelly in prison, and now it looked as if he had taken Megan. Calladine knew he would have to speak to Donnelly again. Livings would complain, and Donnelly would scream persecution. He needed Birch on side. This was too much of a coincidence to let pass.

Joyce came in and Calladine asked, "Has DCI Birch left?"

Joyce looked around as if to make sure no one else was about. "No, sir, but she's got me worried. She's in her office, weeping."

Calladine usually consulted Ruth about such things, but she wasn't here. He looked at Joyce, horrified. Birch weeping! He'd no idea what to do.

Joyce said at once, "You should go and talk to her. She may have had bad news, anything could have happened. You are closer to her than anybody else here."

Calladine snorted. "We're hardly close. All that talking we do is mostly her giving me a bollocking about something or other." He scratched his head. "Do you really think she'd appreciate being disturbed?"

Joyce nodded. "Take her a cup of tea. I'll put the kettle on."

Five minutes later, Calladine knocked on Rhona Birch's door and walked straight in. Joyce had been right. Birch sat behind her desk with a box of tissues and a bottle of malt in front of her, sobbing.

Calladine put the cup in front of her and sat down. "Tea, ma'am. I knew there was something. You've not looked right these last few days."

Birch sniffed. "You're very perceptive, Calladine. I've done my best to keep it to myself but there comes a time . . ."

"Can I help?"

"No. No one can. There is nothing to be done now but wait until . . ."

"What is it, ma'am? Even if I can't do anything it might help to get it off your chest."

He waited while she regarded him doubtfully. Birch was unlike any other woman he knew. Surely it couldn't be man trouble?

Eventually she seemed to come to a decision. "It might surprise you to know that I'm married, Inspector."

Yes it did. He'd had no idea.

Birch poured a generous slug of the whiskey into her tea. "Reg, my husband, is a joiner. Works for himself. We've been separated for years, but we still get on after a fashion. Come together for family stuff and to put on a show for Jack. Jack's our son."

A kid too! "Are you having problems?" Calladine hoped to God she wasn't going to tell him some tricky marital stuff.

"In a manner of speaking. It's Jack. He's gone missing in Australia. He's eighteen and is on a gap year, travelling round the world before he starts university. I had a phone call two days ago. The Australian police have found some of his stuff, including his phone, abandoned in some far-flung place. They've started a search but are not optimistic." She hung her head. "There was evidence of a fight. One of Jack's T-shirts was blood-stained."

Calladine was at a loss. She had a son! He shook his head trying to get the image of a pregnant Birch out of his head. "You never know. It might mean nothing. He'll probably turn up."

"That remains to be seen. They asked for a sample of my DNA to check the blood against. I've sent it off and now I'm going mad sitting here waiting for news."

"Have you considered taking leave?"

Birch nodded. "I'm going to have to. Not knowing what's going on is doing my head in. If Jack doesn't turn up I intend to go out there and help with the investigation." She paused for a moment. "I could be gone for a long time. The force won't like it. I might even have to take early retirement. Give the job up completely."

That shook him. In that instant Calladine realised how much a part of the place Rhona Birch had become. "With any luck it won't come to that. It would be a shame to give up everything you've worked for. You've gelled here, if you know what I mean."

"Good of you to say so, Calladine. I'll admit I have enjoyed my time with the team. You are a good bunch." She poured out more whiskey, offering the bottle to Calladine who shook his head. "Enough of my problems. You don't look too happy yourself."

"My problems are all work-related. Except for the thing with Shez, of course." He placed two images in front of her. "Something odd. This is the individual who visited Donnelly in prison. This is a man caught on CCTV following Megan Heywood this morning. She's currently missing, ma'am."

"It's the same man. No doubt about it."

"Yes, I agree. You know what that means?" Her face fell. "I'm going to have to ask Craig Donnelly about him. We have tried to trace this character ourselves, but no luck. DS Thorpe reckons that's a disguise. So do I."

"Go through his probation officer? Get him to contact Donnelly and deal with Livings. Tell him it's urgent. To do it right away. You can speak to Donnelly tonight." She checked her watch.

"I agree, ma'am. It won't wait."

Calladine made his way back to the incident room. No Ruth or Rocco, and Joyce had gone home. But Imogen was still there.

Calladine picked up the phone. "We need to speak to Donnelly urgently. Look at these." He put the images in front of her. "He visited Donnelly in prison, and here he is following Megan. Odd coincidence, don't you think?"

"Does this mean that there is a connection to Donnelly?"

"It looks like it."

Five tricky minutes on the phone later, a meeting was set up at the vicarage for seven that evening. Joe Rushton would be there — and Livings, of course.

CHAPTER 12

"Doctor Hartley has gone home, Ruth. Was it important?"

Ruth groaned and sat down in the waiting room. "It is really, doc. I wanted some information about a patient."

Doctor Sebastian Hoyle pulled a face. "I'm surprised he agreed. He isn't usually very forthcoming. Patient confidentiality, you know."

"This particular patient is dead, doc. She was murdered."

The doctor's face fell. "Come through to my room. Perhaps I can help."

Ruth was relieved. Doc Hoyle would do what he could. He appreciated what they were up against. He'd been the hospital pathologist until his retirement and had worked closely with Calladine and the team. He'd decided to call it a day when the station had started outsourcing pathology and forensics to the Duggan. Currently he was working part-time as a GP in Leesdon Health Centre. The work evidently suited him. Ruth hadn't seen him looking so well in quite a while.

"That's good of you. It won't get you into bother, will it?"

"No. In cases like this, the information we give out is discretionary." He winked. "And I'm not as discreet as some of my colleagues."

"You like it here, don't you?"

"It suits me fine. The hours are great and it's local."

"You've been here a while now."

"I fit in. Can't do without me now. What's the patient's name?"

"Elsa Ramsden. She lived on Circle Road. Eighteen years old."

Ruth waited while the doc tapped away at his computer. A couple of minutes later, he had Elsa's medical record in front of him.

"I want to know if she was ever pregnant."

"Yes, she was, six months ago. She had a termination and then went on the pill."

"Anything there about who the father was?"

He read through the notes. "No, nothing, Ruth."

"That's a shame. It might have helped." Ruth suspected that Liam Peach was the father. No one was aware of Elsa seeing anyone else, apart from the 'virtual' Aiden.

"She was taking a lot of medication, poor girl. She had a number of allergies. Notably to cats. According to her notes, she only had to come within a few feet of one to have an asthma attack."

"One of my neighbour's kids is the same. It's quite common, isn't it?"

"Yes, but Elsa's reaction was extreme. Cat hair and mould spores affected her badly."

"Thanks, doc. That could be very useful. I'll tell Julian first thing."

"How's your infant?"

"He's great, thanks. I'm on my way now to pick him up from nursery and take him home."

* * *

But Jake had beaten her to the nursery by ten minutes. Now there was just the question of what to have for tea. Her head was too full of the case to remember what might be in the fridge, so she took a quick run round to the supermarket. A few minutes later she had a bagful of pizza and salad. Sorted.

Jake kissed her cheek as he took the shopping bag from her. "That was some day. Those girls never let up. Megan's disappearing act has got them all on edge."

"I'm not surprised. Given what happened to Elsa, it's got us pretty worried too." She took her son off the hearth rug, and popped him in his playpen. "I brought some food."

"I've already put that steak pie you made in the oven. I thought we'd have that with some chips."

Ruth nodded. "Okay, stash the pizza for another day." She started to clear some of the clutter from the living-room floor. It was all still there from this morning. Jake had simply put Harry down amidst it all. She used to live such an orderly life, and now she wondered if she'd ever get it back. "You need to tell the kids to be careful. They should go around in pairs or in a group. We will catch him but we've got nothing as yet."

"I already have. I'm expecting fireworks. Sooner or later the press will get wind of Megan's disappearance and then the whole town will be a bag of nerves. The kids are on edge as it is."

"Jake, if Robert doesn't come back, we're going to be in a fix. Have you made contact? Considered talking to him?"

"What can I do? It's up to him to decide if he has the temperament or not. His timetable needs covering. According to the head we can't get a stand-in until next month. It's the after-school sessions for the A-level students that'll be the worst. Robert was scheduled to do them all, four late ones a week."

So things weren't going to get any better. Ruth was beginning to feel desperate. "So that's down to you now? It doesn't help our situation, does it? I was counting on you to pick Harry up from nursery."

Jake's reply was unconvincing. "I'll try and sort something out."

Ruth flicked her dark hair out of her eyes. "This isn't working, is it? I've only gone back today and already we're knee deep in problems."

"He can stay on at the nursery. It'll only mean another hour or so. Harry will be fine."

That wasn't what Ruth had wanted. Why have a child if all you did was palm him off on the nursery? This situation called for some hard thinking.

The front door bell rang.

Ruth peered out through the front window. "You expecting anyone? I don't recognise the car."

Jake went to answer it and returned with Robert Clarke at his heels.

Clarke looked at Ruth and smiled. "I won't stay. I'm sorry about today, Jake. I've been stupid. All that ribbing from the kids just got to me. It made me wonder what I was doing with my life. But after sitting alone all day in that awful place I'm living in, I began to see what an idiot I've been."

Jake frowned. "So what have you decided?"

Ruth stood and watched, hoping. Right now she needed Jake here, not filling in for absent staff.

"I want to give the job another go."

Ruth felt a wave of relief. "Good for you! Don't let the little buggers grind you down."

Clarke looked embarrassed. "I didn't expect it to be so grim. The thing with that sixth form group really messed with my head."

Ruth had gone back to tidying up. "You're young. They probably fancy you." He wasn't bad-looking actually. Tall, with broad shoulders and floppy dark hair, a bit like Jake. "That'll be what's at the bottom of it."

Jake shook his head.

"You're not local, are you? What brought you up here?" Ruth said.

"I did my degree at Manchester, and teacher training in Huddersfield."

"Didn't you fancy a job back home?"

He shook his head. He didn't say why. And he didn't say where home was either.

"Want to stay for a bite to eat?" Jake said.

Ruth could have killed him. The house was a mess and they had a shedload of stuff to do. Besides which, she doubted the pie would stretch three ways.

"Thanks, but no. I'm off to view a new flat out Hopecross way. It's pleasant there, rural and quiet."

"You'll be in tomorrow?" asked Jake.

"Bright and early," Clarke promised.

"Did he really have to call for help?" Ruth asked when he'd left. "The girls said something about it when I spoke to them."

"He was having a particularly bad day. The girls had it in for him. They didn't fancy doing the work he'd set them so they had a go instead. But it wasn't as bad as they made out. He didn't threaten Elsa. Not his style."

"What do you think of his chances now?"

"He's got his head together from the sound of it. He'll be fine."

Ruth wasn't so sure. "I think he's hiding something. He's evasive about his past. Keep an eye on him, that's my advice."

* * *

Michael Livings glared at them. "That's twice today you've interviewed Craig. It's a damned intrusion. I don't know what you think he can tell you."

Joe Rushton shuffled uneasily. They stood in the hallway, just inside the door, and obviously weren't going to be invited any further.

Calladine tried to appease the man. "I'd like Craig to look at a couple of photos, that's all. It isn't an interview. But I do think he might be able to help with our investigations."

Livings scoffed. "I know what that means, Inspector. Next thing you'll be dragging him down to the police station again. Well, it isn't happening!"

Craig Donnelly emerged from what appeared to be the kitchen. He nodded at Rushton but ignored Calladine.

Calladine showed him the image from the prison camera. "Do you know this man?"

"You know I do. We both know where that was taken — in Strangeways. It's Jason."

"How do you know him, Craig?"

"He wrote to me a couple of months before I got out. Said he was doing research and asked if I'd speak to him. I sent him a visiting order and he came a few times. We talked a bit, that was all."

"What about?"

"Prison life mostly."

"Did he ask about Annabelle Roper?"

"After a while he did. Turned out the man was obsessed. Wanted to know how I'd done it, what I'd done to her and what it had felt like. Bloody pervert. I told him I was innocent." He cast a look at the vicar. "But he wasn't having any. In the end I refused to see him. He wasn't right in the head. He wrote to me a couple of times after that, but I burnt the letters. Filthy stuff, he wrote. Turned my stomach."

That was rich coming from Donnelly! "Why didn't you say something? Alert the prison authorities?"

"Didn't see how it would help."

"How did he react when you told him you hadn't done it?" said Calladine.

"He didn't believe me. No one has ever believed me."

Livings made a tutting sound. "You didn't tell me any of this. If this Jason chap was bothering you, I would have helped."

"He was a nutter. I dealt with him. I haven't seen him since. End of."

"How did you deal with him, Craig?" asked Calladine.

104

"I told him to sling his hook, copper. I threatened him. He had no idea who I knew on the outside. I said if he bothered me again, I'd have him done over. I was joking, of course."

The vicar made more tutting noises.

Calladine showed Donnelly the second image. "This was captured by CCTV earlier this morning in Leesdon. The girl is missing. I'd say it was the same man, wouldn't you?"

Reverend Livings jumped in. "What are you getting at, Inspector? This really is bad form. If you are suggesting that Craig has anything to do with this, you're wrong."

"I'm not suggesting anything. But I need to know more about this man. I think he's dangerous. He may well be the last person to have seen the poor girl alive."

"You think he's killed her?" Donnelly's eyes slid anxiously from Livings to Calladine.

"Has he contacted you since you got out, Craig?" Calladine asked. He'd seen that look before, the fear in his eyes. Donnelly had looked the same all those years ago when he was being questioned about Annabelle. He was not a good liar.

Craig Donnelly shook his head. His eyes were on the floor now. "No, and I haven't seen him around either. No reason I should. He isn't from round here."

"Jason Kent is not his real name, and the get-up is a disguise. When you met him in person, did you realise that?"

"No. I just saw someone struggling to get by. He arrived at Strangeways on the bus, and didn't even have money for the coffee machine. He was just as he looks there."

Calladine was frustrated. This was a waste of time. "Is there nothing you can add? A girl's life may depend on it." He was hoping that Livings might bring his influence to bear. But he said nothing.

Donnelly shook his head. Calladine was convinced he was holding something back. They both were, he and Livings. Throughout their chat Donnelly had been far too shifty. Calladine would have loved to take Donnelly by his scrawny neck and shake the truth out of him.

By the time Calladine left the vicarage he'd had enough. He wanted to check in with Shez, see how she was holding up. But he had to speak to Megan's mum first. The woman would be going out of her mind.

It was only a short walk from the leafy lane where the vicarage was situated to the concrete monstrosity that was the Hobfield. Cutting across the square, with the tower blocks looming above him, Calladine made his way onto Circle Road. There was already a police car outside Megan's house.

Megan's mother was on the doorstep. "Have you found her?"

Calladine shook his head. "No, not yet. When did you hear from her last?"

"This morning. I heard her moving about in her room. I said she was to stay put, but she didn't listen. Now look what's happened. Megan knew she'd be next. She said as much herself."

"You haven't spoken to her today?"

"No, but that's usual. When I got back from work and found she wasn't here I was angry. I knew she'd gone to school, her uniform was missing. I rang her mobile but it was dead. I contacted the school and they said Megan hadn't been in." She was weeping, her voice trembling. "I got that call from you lot and I knew. He's got her, hasn't he?"

CHAPTER 13

Thursday

The early morning was Calladine's favourite time of day. Leesdon was quiet as he walked to the police station. A shower of rain had freshened the streets. The takeaways were shut, so the streets were free of their usual odour of chip fat and kebab.

He was first in. There was a lot to do, but first he wanted hot coffee. It would help him think. They had one dead girl, and another was missing, but the incident board was almost empty. The team needed to focus. With luck the forensic results and Elsa Ramsden's phone records would be in today. They might yield that much-needed breakthrough. Megan's laptop was already at the Duggan.

Imogen arrived next. "Morning, guv."

The first thing she did was switch on her computer. The younger members of his team didn't seem to be able to function without a keyboard at their fingertips. Unlike Calladine.

Computer running, Imogen said, "Julian wants to speak to you."

Calladine wondered whether this message came via email or was relayed over breakfast. "How are the two of you doing in that new house of yours?"

"I love it. Despite originally wanting something entirely different, I like living on a modern development. We've got lots of young neighbours, plenty going on."

"Julian?"

"Not so thrilled. He says there's too *much* going on. You know what he's like, a serious sod with a single topic of conversation."

"He's a brilliant forensic scientist. We need more like him."

Imogen grinned. "For God's sake don't tell him that. There'll be no living with him."

Next, Rocco came in. He and Imogen swapped chitchat about the previous evening until Ruth turned up.

"Sorry, gang. Same old story. Wouldn't eat his breakfast then threw up as I pulled up at the nursery. I think he's sickening for something."

"Jake?"

She chucked a pencil at a smirking Rocco. "No! Harry, you plank!"

Calladine announced the morning briefing, with a serious edge to his voice. He paced the floor with his hands in his trouser pockets. "Get what you need and pin back your ears. This case needs a bomb putting under it. We need to sort this and quick. We are no nearer solving the Elsa Ramsden murder and now Megan Heywood is missing. That gives me a very bad feeling. We're in here, drinking coffee and taking the piss while she's out there somewhere, in heaven knows what danger."

The team looked at each other. He was on one, but he was right.

Ruth began. "I've been thinking about the motive. Who would want to kill a teenage girl? I know they can be hard work — Jake complains enough. We should look again at what links them."

"School; that online stalker, Aiden; and a dislike of Gaby Donnelly," Rocco said.

Ruth looked at the others. "Do we have anything more on this Aiden? He chatted up the girls, going from one to the other. Megan said he'd dumped Elsa and moved onto her. It was then that Elsa went missing. I'm wondering if he's moved on again. Chosen his next victim and done for Megan."

Calladine was on it immediately. "Donnelly! This was how he operated the last time. Not online, but he'll have learned a thing or two inside. I spoke to him last night. He was evasive. Hid behind the vicar. He has to be top of our list, surely?"

"He can account for his actions. That diary he keeps, remember? He's working for that vicar helping local residents. They can vouch for him. I don't see how Donnelly would have the time," Ruth demurred.

Calladine went on, "I want you all to look for any link, no matter how tenuous, between Donnelly and those girls. We know about Peach. He went out with both Elsa and Megan. But what else is there? And be aware that he's working with someone else. Jason Kent, the man who visited him in prison, has been seen on CCTV here in Leesdon, and in the same place, at the same time, as Megan. I don't believe he'd come here and not seek Donnelly out. But Donnelly has denied seeing him. According to him, this character was fascinated by the Annabelle Roper killing. We need to find Kent fast. I don't think that will be easy. He's clear enough in the images but both Thorpe and I reckon that's a disguise." He passed copies of the images to the team.

Imogen looked at the pictures. "Even so, if this is how he's going about, we should pass it on to uniform. They might spot him."

"He looks as if he's living rough. We could check the hostels," added Rocco.

Calladine nodded. "Okay, circulate the image. See what comes back." He stood by the incident board, a marker in his hand.

"Both Elsa and Megan were being chatted up online by this charmer, Aiden. He has to be in the frame," Ruth said.

Calladine started writing. "Pity we don't know who he really is then. Imogen — chase the Duggan for more on that one. We could do with a location at the very least. Your IT wiz might have a lead on that by now."

"We still haven't spoken to Gaby Donnelly," said Ruth.

"We'll do that today. We'll speak to Rachel Hayes too."

"Have you looked at that notebook of Donnelly's, sir?" asked Rocco.

"Yes, it's all pretty mundane. I've passed a couple of queries onto uniform but it all appears to check out."

Imogen looked up from her computer screen. "Julian has sent the interim forensic report through. He says will you ring him, it's urgent."

"I suggest you give it a look over before we go any further. I'll see what Julian wants." Calladine went into his office, closed the door behind him and, still on his feet, called Julian. He couldn't settle. "Julian, what is it?"

"I think you'll be pleased. You have the report, most of which I or Natasha have already relayed verbally. I'm still conducting tests on the girl's hair. But we did find something. Among the detritus in the dustbin was a pair of earrings. There was a tiny smear of blood on one of them which does not belong to Elsa Ramsden. It doesn't have the same DNA profile."

Calladine held his breath. Was this the much-needed breakthrough?

"The blood belongs to one Craig Donnelly. An individual you know, I believe."

"You're sure, Julian?"

"I know my job, Tom. Donnelly's DNA is on record."

"So the bastard did kill her! Up to his old tricks, just as I thought."

"That is a possibility." There was a pause at the end of the line. "Although things are not always as they seem. Blood on one of Elsa's earrings alone may not be enough. There was some hair wrapped around the earring. We're testing it to make sure it's Elsa's. But, apart from that, we could not find any of Elsa's DNA. Odd, if she'd been wearing the earrings. Also there are differences between this killing and that of Annabelle Roper."

"Did you find anything else?"

"No. I've emailed you an enlarged image of the earrings."

"Thanks, Julian. I'll tell the team the good news."

Calladine was jubilant. He'd put this down to Donnelly right from the start. The earrings had to belong to Elsa. Why else would they have been found with the body? He went back into the incident room and wrote the name in huge letters across the incident board. "His blood on an earring found in that bin along with Elsa's body. I want him bringing in — now!"

* * *

"Donnelly, it's me. I need a place to stash some stuff. It can't stay here. I've had the police sniffing around." Peach sounded anxious.

"There's nothing I can do, Peachy. You know how things are. You'll have to go somewhere else."

"You have to help. There is no one else. I'll make it worth your while."

"I'm busy. I've got jobs to do for Livings. They'll take me the rest of the day. I haven't got time to mess around with you."

"What's happened to you? Tell the barmy God-botherer to do one. I warned you what it'd be like before you got out. Don't listen, that's your problem."

"Get off my back. I've warned you before. Keep out of my life."

"Perhaps I should have a word with the good vicar."

"Do that and it'll be your death warrant." He meant it. Donnelly didn't want anyone or anything spoiling what he had. "I won't do anything to annoy him. He's given me a home and a job. If Livings sees you hanging around here he'll go to the police. He trusts me, and I owe him."

"You owe me too. Or have you forgotten about that? I did you a huge favour not long ago, took risks. So far I've had nothing in return."

"You'll get yours. You need to be patient. Meanwhile, I won't have Livings rattled. It's down to him that I'm out."

"In my book you owe me double what you owe him. Have you forgotten what I did for you?" Donnelly didn't reply. "I need a safe place for a short while. You can sort it, given that huge rambling pile you live in."

Donnelly didn't like it, but he'd have to help Peachy. He was a loose cannon. For now, there was more to be gained by keeping him sweet. "I'll leave the van unlocked. It's parked by the side gate. Put it in the back, under the tarpaulin."

"Thanks, Craig."

"What's in the package?"

"Better if you don't know."

"Dodgy then. The police keep asking me about you. They've been round here too. What if they come back?"

"All you have to do is keep your mouth shut."

"So what is it? Drugs?"

"I need the money."

"Who do you owe?"

"Keep out of it. Safer that way."

"I'm not doing this for nothing."

"I'll give you a ton. I'll leave it with the package. But no questions, and don't blab to anyone. Understand?"

"The drugs — stolen are they? If you're willing to part with a ton then someone's looking."

"No one's looking. Hide the stuff and don't breathe a word."

"So why pay me so much?"

"I'm paying you a ton so you don't ask stupid questions. Just keep your bloody mouth shut! I'll be in touch again when I need to pick the stuff up."

Conversation ended, Donnelly pocketed his mobile and walked into the graveyard. At the far end, sheltered by a high hedge and down half a dozen steep steps was a vault belonging to the Brayshaw family. It was nearly one hundred and fifty years old. At one time the Brayshaws had been the wealthiest folk in the area. In the nineteenth century, Ernest Brayshaw had owned a cotton mill in Oldston, and had made a fortune. None of the family was left, so the church was left to maintain the vault.

Donnelly had looked the vault over. But decided not to start any maintenance for now — except for fitting a new lock. The place could prove useful. He'd been inside a couple of times to sweep up the leaves and other rubbish that had collected over the years. He hadn't looked too closely, but he reckoned there were at least six coffins in the vault. The vicar had not been near it for years, and neither had anyone else. It was the perfect hiding place.

Donnelly inhaled the fresh morning air. This transaction did have its compensations. A ton was good. He'd buy something nice for Gaby. Try to get her back on side.

* * *

First to reach the vicarage were two police cars full of uniformed officers. Within seconds Michael Livings was peering out of the door. He was about to tackle them when Calladine's car pulled up.

"Donnelly. Where is he?"

"Working, Inspector. What is it now?"

"Working where?"

"He's round the back in the churchyard helping David cut the grass."

"Go and get him," Calladine ordered.

"This is getting so regular it's laughable. You drag Craig in, you learn nothing and then you let him go. I'd have thought you had better things to do with your time."

The officers returned minutes later with Donnelly in tow. Despite the handcuffs, he was struggling.

"Craig Donnelly, you are under arrest for the murder of Elsa Ramsden." Calladine read him his rights and led him to the car.

Livings said nothing. His eyes were blazing, but his mouth remained firmly shut.

Calladine grinned. "What's wrong, vicar? Cat got your tongue? That reminds me. Have you got a cat here, by the way?"

Livings stared at Calladine. "We have two. They're not pets. They earn their keep. We need them to keep the mice down."

"Make sure you get a sample of cat hair," Calladine told one of the crime scene officers.

Once Calladine was back in the car, Ruth gave him a concerned look. "I hope you're right about this, otherwise Livings will have your hide."

"We've got his DNA on one of Elsa's earrings. That not good enough for you?"

"But no DNA of Elsa's. It doesn't feel right to me. I know what we've got. It may or may not hold up in court. Depends on how good Donnelly's lawyer is. For me it's a little too convenient. How come we find *two* earrings but nothing else?"

"They must have come off the body when she was dumped."

"Both of them? Like I said — convenient."

"She was naked. He'd removed everything. She had no clothes, bar the tie, and no jewellery."

"So why leave the earrings behind, Tom? It doesn't make sense. And one of them smeared with Donnelly's blood, left for us to find."

"You think it was left there deliberately?"

"A stitch-up — could be. But it poses questions. Try to answer them and you begin to see the puzzle."

Calladine decided to ignore this. "We need to get him back fast. Megan may still be alive. There has been no body found yet."

Ruth sighed. "I do hope you are right on this one, Tom. I don't want to think what Donnelly's legal crew will do to you if you're not."

They pulled into the station car park. "That's not going to happen."

Calladine called over to the uniformed officer holding Donnelly. "Get him processed and stick him in a cell." He turned to Ruth. "Do you want in on this one?"

"Someone has to get your back."

CHAPTER 14

"SOCOs are at Donnelly's cottage now, ma'am."

"Given what you've got, I was happy to sanction the search warrant. But it must only be the cottage, understand? We have no reason to look at the vicarage itself. Livings has not done anything wrong. I have a bad feeling about this, Calladine. Livings will take us to hell and back if we're wrong."

"We're sure to find more, ma'am. We haven't found Elsa's clothes, her phone, or her . . . tongue." Calladine shuddered.

Birch looked thoughtful. "A trophy taker. Do you want me to join you in the interview?"

"Sergeant Bayliss and I can manage, ma'am."

"Okay, but I'll be watching. And for God's sake don't lose it. By the book, Calladine."

Calladine ignored her comment, but that didn't stop it resounding through his head. As far as he was concerned, it would be all too easy to lose it with Donnelly. "Anything on your son?"

"No. I've booked a flight for tomorrow. I can't sit back waiting for phone calls. I need to be there, get stuck in."

"I wish you luck, ma'am. Hope you find him."

Calladine returned to the incident room. He had a quick swig of coffee, nodded to Ruth and they were off. High on adrenalin, he wanted to get this rolling.

"Found your missing model yet?" Ruth asked.

"No. It's not me that's looking for her. That's Thorpe's case."

"Have you considered that it might have something to do with our man?"

"Donnelly? What do you mean?"

"Kate Reynolds walks through town and just disappears. Sound familiar?"

"We'll ask him."

When they entered the incident room, Donnelly was sitting beside his solicitor, whispering to him.

Calladine began. "I've no intention of dragging this out. I want to know where Megan Heywood is."

"How should I know? I don't even know who she is."

Calladine put a photo of her on the desk for them to see. "This is Megan. Young — a teenager — and blonde. Exactly how you like them, in fact."

"No comment."

"If you're going to go down that route, Craig, we'll get nowhere. And I'll get annoyed."

"I've never seen her before."

"Try this girl then, Elsa Ramsden."

"I don't know her either. You're wasting your time and mine. You're becoming a right pain in the arse, copper."

"You do know Elsa. You took her, imprisoned her and then killed her. Not content with that, you put her in a wheelie bin, just like with Annabelle. We have proof." Calladine took the photo of Elsa's earrings and placed it in front of Donnelly and his solicitor. "These were found in the same bin."

Donnelly shrugged. "So? What's it got to do with me?"

"One of them has got your blood on it. Can you explain that, Craig?"

Craig Donnelly went pale. He gripped the edge of the table and his knuckles were white.

"How did you get that scrape on your hand, Craig?"

"I've been digging the gardens of half the folk in this town for the last few weeks, that's how. This can't be happening, not again." He turned to his solicitor and shook his head. "Last time it was a damned necklace and a shoe. Now this. I'm being set up, just like before."

Calladine leaned back in his chair. "I very much doubt that, Craig. I'll ask you again. Where is Megan Heywood? What have you done with her?"

"And I'm telling you, copper, I don't know her. I'm not stupid. I can see what this looks like, but I'm telling the truth. This is not down to me." He tapped the photo of the earrings, then turned to his solicitor. "I don't feel right."

"That character who visited you in prison, Jason Kent. He has been seen in Leesdon. Does he take them for you? Are you in this together?"

Donnelly was sweating. His eyes were blazing with anxiety and rage.

"My client needs a break. This has come as a complete shock to him," the solicitor said.

Calladine thumped his fist on the table. "Shock? How do you imagine the families of those girls are feeling? Tell me what you've done with Megan and you can have all the rest you need!"

Donnelly groaned, and rubbed at his chest. "I can't breathe," he gasped.

"We have forensic evidence. We will find Kent. Why not cut your losses, Craig, and tell me where Megan is?" Calladine stood up.

"My chest hurts. I'm in pain."

"Get him a doctor!" Calladine stalked out of the interview room.

"That went well. I did warn you."

He really didn't need Birch's sarcasm now. "I'm doing my best, ma'am, in the only way I know how. That bastard is putting it on. He did this the last time, on the Roper case. Threw a wobble and got carted off to hospital. There was bugger all wrong then, and it'll be the same this time."

"See what the doctor says. If he's okay, give him an hour or so to calm down before you start again."

Calladine made his way back to the incident room. He was furious. The longer Donnelly held out, the less chance they had of finding Megan alive.

"I'm going for a word with Elsa's mum," Ruth announced. "Just crossing the t's."

"Want company?"

"Not yours, I don't. I'll take Rocco." Ruth nodded at the young DC.

Calladine disappeared into his office, slamming the door behind him. This case was not getting any easier.

* * *

What's on your mind?"

"Those bloody earrings, Rocco. I can't get them out of my head."

"I don't see why. It's straightforward enough. How could one of them be smeared with Donnelly's blood if he didn't handle it?"

Ruth scoffed. "You're not that stupid. It's far too convenient. We've got nothing else belonging to Elsa. Anyone could have set that up for us to find. Calladine is desperate to pin it on Donnelly, God knows why. I'm not entirely sure the man was guilty first time round."

"Calladine won't want to hear that."

"Tell me about it. I've already voiced my opinions. Which is why I don't think he's entirely happy with me at the moment." They were approaching Circle Road. There was a group of people standing around outside the Ramsden house. "The press. We'll have to keep our heads down. And no matter what we're told, not a word," she warned Rocco.

Running the gauntlet of voice recorders and cameras, Ruth and Rocco kept their sights on the front door. Elsa's mum had spotted them. She opened it a few inches and the detectives slipped inside.

"Load of rubbish the lot of them. All they want is a story. A bit of tittle-tattle to put in the bloody papers. They're not bothered about my girl, or the creep that killed her. They keep asking if she had a boyfriend. All they're after is dirt."

"Mrs Ramsden, did Elsa have pierced ears?" Ruth got straight to the point. Calladine would drag Donnelly back into that interview room within the hour, so they didn't have long.

"One of them was."

"She had only one pierced ear?"

"She'd had them both pierced years ago. But she only ever wore the one earring. In her left ear. She told me the other one had healed up."

So much for finding a pair. "Can you tell me if these were hers?"

The woman studied the image for a few seconds and shook her head. "No, definitely not. Those are those loop things. My Elsa preferred a single stud. For the last few months she was wearing one huge red thing."

"You're quite sure? She didn't wear a pair?"

"No, just the one. She never got round to having the right one done again. Besides, she'd never wear anything like those. Here, I'll show you." She led the way upstairs to Elsa's bedroom and opened a jewellery box. "All neatly in a row, and all the same. Red studs, her favourites."

"Are you sure a friend or relative didn't give her these as a present?"

"Positive. They're just not her thing. She wouldn't even wear the left one. This bedroom might be all pink and frilly but underneath Elsa was a bit of a Goth. Black and red were what she liked to wear. Not those tiny bits of metal. They say nowt, not distinctive enough."

"And they're not yours?" Rocco asked.

Mrs Ramsden flicked her hair back. "I don't have pierced ears, son."

"Thanks, you've been a great help."

As they went down the stairs Elsa's mother said, "Word's out you've got him. Make sure he suffers for what he did to my Elsa. Evil bastard!"

Back in the car Ruth rang Julian Batho at the Duggan.

"Julian, would you check Elsa Ramsden's body again? It's those earrings you found. According to her mother she only wore one, and always in her left ear. The right lobe was pierced, but had healed up."

"Is she sure?"

"Yes, positive, and they are not what Elsa would have worn anyway. Elsa favoured those large studs. Check both lobes again, will you?"

"Very well. I'll check and get back."

Ruth continued. "The DNA you found — Donnelly's but none belonging to Elsa? Isn't that a bit odd?"

"It could be seen that way. But as I told Tom, there was hair caught in one of them. It was Elsa's."

"Okay, I'll wait for your call back at the nick."

"I don't see how having only one pierced ear helps us," Rocco admitted.

"They found a pair. I'm guessing we are supposed to think that Elsa lost them when she was put in the bin. Whoever set that up didn't know enough about Elsa. He hadn't checked her ears and seen that she only wore one."

Rocco checked his watch. "The hour's almost up."

"Better hurry then, before Calladine makes an even bigger ass of himself."

* * *

"Donnelly's been checked over and he's fine. He had a panic attack," the police doctor told Calladine. "I've given him something to calm him down."

"I'll give him a bloody panic attack! He's playing for time." The office phone rang. It was Julian for Ruth. "She's gone haring off somewhere with Rocco. I can give her a message," Calladine said.

"She asked about Elsa's ears. When she gets back, tell her she was right," Julian said.

"Care to elaborate?"

"Only one of Elsa's ears was pierced. The other one had healed over. Apparently she only wore those large stud things. Ruth asked me to look at the body again. The left lobe has an enlarged hole for an earring, and in the right ear, nothing. It would appear that the ones we found did not belong to the girl."

"What does it mean?"

"On its own, who knows? But Elsa's mother also told Ruth that the earrings we found did not belong to her daughter. More than likely those in the bin were not the murdered girl's. Given Ruth's information, I'm doing further tests on the hair we found to make sure."

Calladine slammed the phone down. This was not what he wanted to hear. Donnelly was set to wriggle free yet again. Just then, Ruth and Rocco returned. "What exactly have you been up to?" asked Calladine.

Ruth held up the photo of the earrings. "We've been to ask Elsa's mum about these. Like we should have done before we dragged Donnelly in here. She says they are not Elsa's. Not her style. Elsa only ever wore large studs, and only one of them. Here, a class photo from Jake. See?" She pointed to Elsa. "Like a bloody beacon in her ear."

"You're saying they were placed there?"

"I'm saying we investigate, and make absolutely sure before we go any further with Donnelly. The press know we've arrested him. There'll be all sorts of flak if they get the merest whiff that we got it wrong."

Calladine flopped down on Ruth's chair. "The fact remains that there are earrings and one of them does have Donnelly's blood on it."

"But they are not Elsa's. Someone wants us to go after Donnelly. Why? I have no idea."

"So what do we do?"

"We speak to him — nicely."

"You coming back in with me?"

Ruth looked at him fondly. "I think I better had, don't you? Let me do the talking this time."

"I've let him get to me, I admit it. I wanted Donnelly to go down for this. In my head I'm back dealing with the Roper case. Seeing Elsa Ramsden like that, it's affected my judgement."

"This is not the same case, Tom. I don't think Donnelly did kill Elsa. I think someone wants us to think he did and is planting evidence."

"Why?"

"As I said, I've no idea. But you have to admit, Donnelly is a convenient scapegoat."

Calladine looked at her. "That man Kent?"

"We need to find him. Anything come in from uniform?" Ruth asked Imogen.

"Nothing. All hostels checked and I'm having another look at the CCTV from around the town."

CHAPTER 15

Calladine's voice was level, and he even managed a small smile. "He visited you several times in prison. You do know him, Craig, or why would he bother? Tell us about him. It might save a young girl's life. If you won't talk because he's threatened you, we can help."

Donnelly looked at Ruth, then nodded to Calladine. He smirked. "Muzzled him, have you? Realised his heavy-handed tactics won't get him anywhere. About bloody time."

"We only want the truth, Craig. If you do know where Kent is, or you can help us to find him, we will be grateful," Ruth said.

"A few soft words from you won't make any difference either, love." He picked up the image. "I don't know him. Sure, he visited. He did a lot of talking, but I wasn't interested. In the end he gave up. I haven't seen him since."

"What did he talk about?" Calladine asked.

"I told you. The girl. He went on about the murder, nothing else."

"Didn't you find that strange?" asked Ruth.

"He was just another nutter. I got letters from all sorts of folk. Destroyed them."

"Have you seen or contacted him since you've been back in Leesdon?"

He looked at Calladine. "I already said I hadn't. Why would I? I know nothing about the man."

"Did he ever mention a man called Aiden to you, Craig?" asked Ruth.

"No."

Ruth told him, "We found an earring with your blood on it by the girl's body. We believe that someone is trying to fit you up." She gave him a moment to consider this. "Want to help us now, Craig?"

"No, love. I know nothing about any Aiden, I haven't seen Kent and I've no idea how my blood got on them damn earrings."

Calladine shook his head. "I don't believe you, Craig. I think you have seen Kent. He's not local, no one knows him, yet he's been seen in Leesdon. Why would he come here, except to see you?"

There was a knock. Rocco stuck his head round the door and beckoned to Calladine. He looked agitated.

"Sorry to interrupt, sir, but it's urgent. Kate Reynolds, sir. The chap in the ticket office remembers her. She had to search through her bag for her pass. Took ages, made him late going off shift. He says Kate left the station alone but when she reached the road outside she was accosted by a bloke with long, untidy hair and a full beard. I showed him the image of Jason Kent and he was pretty sure it was him. If he's right, then the cases are linked."

"Good work, Rocco. But there is a ransom demand for Kate. Nothing like that with the girls."

"Perhaps he thinks Kate has money," Rocco suggested.

"We have to find him. I'm convinced that bastard in there knows who this joker is, but he's saying nothing."

"They could be in it together, sir. Kent does the taking, Donnelly the rest."

Calladine wasn't sure. "In that case, how does he slip away to deal with the girls? The vicar is on his back all the time. Then there are the online meetings. Does Donnelly have access to a computer?"

"Donnelly is doing jobs around town for all and sundry. He's out in that van of the vicar's on a daily basis. He could be up to anything."

Rocco was right. "That cottage of his. Tell the search team to be sure to do a thorough job. There must be a phone hidden somewhere, and if there is a computer, tell them to bring it in. If Donnelly and Kent are working together, they must communicate somehow."

Calladine returned to the interview room. "Jason Kent. You can stop pissing us about now, Craig. You have seen him recently, haven't you?"

"Why do you keep asking me about him? You're like a dog with a bone, you are. He visited me in Strangeways. Apart from that — nothing."

"I don't believe you. The pair of you are in this together. He does things for you. Takes the girls off the streets for a start. Usually on their way to school. How does he manage that, in broad daylight?"

"Whatever he does has nothing to do with me." Donnelly looked at his solicitor. "How long is this going to go on for? I can't take much more. This copper has a one-track mind."

Calladine showed him the photo of Kate. "Do you know this young woman, Craig?"

Donnelly gave a long, low whistle. "She's a real looker. No schoolgirl either, Inspector."

"No, but she has been taken like the others. And by this character." Calladine tapped the Jason Kent photo. "I'll ask again, do you know where he is?"

"Can't say I do. But I wouldn't mind introducing to the girl." Donnelly grinned.

This was getting them nowhere. After the sedative he'd been given, Donnelly was so relaxed he was positively flippant.

Ruth tried again. "Do you know where Kent lives, Craig?"

"No, but I know he's not local."

"Why do you say that?"

"His accent isn't right. I'd say he's lived round here, but he's from somewhere else."

"Are you sure you haven't seen him since you've been back?"

"Positive."

Calladine gave up on Kent. "Tell us about your relationship with Liam Peach."

"I have nothing to do with him. Can't think when I saw him last."

"You used to be friends. What happened?"

"We fell out. Now he keeps away. That suits me fine."

"What did you fall out about?"

"It's a long time ago. I can't remember."

"That was some beating he gave you before you were arrested for the Annabelle Roper murder. Do you remember why he did that?"

"Look, copper, I'm sick of this. That was years ago. It could have been about anything."

"I am surprised you can't elaborate. You were black and blue, Craig. I'm sure I'd remember what it'd been about if someone had done that to me."

Rocco was back. "A word, sir." Calladine followed him out into the corridor.

"Julian's been on. There is a problem. The hair found wrapped around the earring. It was freshly washed and even had traces of conditioner on it."

"So?"

"The hair on Elsa's body was very dirty. She'd been locked up. Her hair had picked up all sorts from wherever she'd been kept. Julian reckons that even if the earrings were hers and had become dislodged, any hair with them should have been dirty, covered in smoke particles and grime like the rest of it. They weren't. So something is wrong."

"But it is Elsa's hair?"

"Julian is double checking."

"So the damn things were placed. Daubed with Donnelly's blood and deliberately left for us to find. Someone went to a lot of trouble, but why, and who?"

"Someone who wants him back behind bars," Rocco suggested.

"So what have we got?"

"Without the earrings — nothing, sir," Rocco replied.

Calladine paced the corridor. "We've got bugger all. I'm going to have to let the creep go — again!"

Donnelly didn't say much as he left, but his solicitor made it quite clear that this was harassment and he intended to take it further on his client's behalf.

"Not your finest hour, Calladine," Birch said.

"No, ma'am."

Birch's face was like thunder. "I've had the ACC on. You must not go near Donnelly again unless you have proof positive, checked, double checked and run past me, or my replacement. Understand?

"Yes, ma'am. Replacement? You are going then. Your boy hasn't turned up?"

"No, he hasn't. I can't sit around here waiting for the phone to ring any longer. I'm off tomorrow. But that does not change anything with regard to Donnelly. Understand this, Calladine. Go after that man again without solid evidence and it could cost you your job. DI Long is back off leave in two days' time. He will be acting DCI for the time being."

Long in the hot seat — again. That'd please him.

"I suggest you go back and re-examine all the data you have. It's time to go after someone else, Calladine. Give Donnelly a rest."

* * *

"They didn't find a computer," Imogen confirmed. "Nothing in Donnelly's cottage and the vicar has stated that he doesn't have one either."

"Mobile phone?"

"Only the one Livings gave Donnelly for work purposes. We're getting a list of calls and texts from the provider. But it's one of the older types, sir, not a smart phone. So he could not have used it to access the internet."

Calladine confronted the team. It was time to tell them about Kate Reynolds. "We have an added complication. One of Shez's girls has been kidnapped. She was seen at Leesdon railway station being followed by a man closely resembling Jason Kent."

"When was this?" Imogen asked.

"Friday, but we've only known she was missing for twenty-four hours."

Ruth summed it up. "Elsa is dead, and Megan and this Kate Reynolds are missing."

"Yes, Ruth. The difference is, a ransom has been demanded for the return of Kate."

"Who reported it?"

"Shez has received a ransom letter and one phone call. He is asking two hundred thousand for her return."

"Our case, guv?" Imogen asked.

"For the time being it's been handed to Thorpe. But the way things are going, it'll more than likely come to us."

"Has anyone spoken to her family?"

"Not yet, Imogen. And that's another complication. Her father is Alan Reynolds. He investigated the Annabelle Roper killing. He's retired these days and not well. If he does know, it'll be tearing him apart."

Ruth looked up. "You know him. Perhaps you should have a word. Try and find out if he's been contacted."

Calladine nodded. He'd been putting it off but it was about time he spoke to Reynolds, and not just about his daughter. "I'll call in on my way home."

Ruth looked at Rocco. "Any joy finding Kent?"

"No. He appears, then melts away. Like Thorpe says, he's a ghost."

"He's wearing a disguise — long coat, the hair and beard. The reality is, he could be anyone," Calladine told them.

"Have we cross-referenced Donnelly's movements with those of Kent's?"

"Not yet, Imogen. Would you look through the notebook and do that?"

"Where are we with forensics?" asked Ruth.

"I'm looking at Elsa's phone records, they came through this afternoon. There are dozens of calls to Megan and Rachel Hayes. She accessed several websites, for music mostly. But nothing that will help us. She didn't ring whoever took her, nor did they text her. The phone went dead on Circle Road. We know that Megan's phone went dead on Byron's Lane. Both are on the route to school. That adds to the theory that both girls were on their way to school when they were taken. Uniform have asked around, but no one saw anything. The problem is, there are no shops or anything else until you get to the High Street," Rocco told them.

Imogen checked her notes. "Elsa's computer is still giving the Duggan problems. Whoever she spoke to online was very good. Covered his tracks like a pro. Julian is still working on Elsa's body. A number of items have been retrieved from Byron's Lane, including a hair bobble. We have a photo of it to show to Megan's mother. It has blood on it, sir. Julian is running tests."

Calladine perched on the edge of Joyce's desk. "What's the betting it turns out to be Donnelly's?"

"If it does, and this isn't down to him, he's getting serious grief from someone," Rocco replied.

Calladine took this up. "And that someone has got himself a sample of Donnelly's blood? Where from? How? And if he has, then the killer has to know Donnelly."

Imogen handed Calladine the office phone. "Julian for you, guv."

"We found grey cat fur in Elsa Ramsden's hair. Persian, to be precise. As you know, the girl was allergic to cats and a number of other things. Given the state of her air passages I'd say the cat had been in close proximity to her for most of her imprisonment."

"So the killer has a cat?"

"Looks that way. The hair trapped in the loop of the earring was Elsa's. However, it had been taken before she died. There isn't much but the individual hairs look freshly cut."

"Clippings from the hairdressers?"

"Could be. She hadn't eaten for twenty-four hours or so, but she had been given a cocktail of drugs — tranquilisers washed down with milk, and we found puncture marks in her arm from injections of morphine. The blood on the note was Elsa's too. The note was hand-written on a scrap torn from a sheet of printer paper. The pen — a common or garden biro."

"Do we have an image of the note left in the Annabelle Roper killing? The words were the same. I'm thinking about comparing the writing."

"I'll see what I can do."

"Thanks, Julian."

"Anything useful?" asked Ruth.

"Our killer has a cat. A long-haired Persian type. There are cats at the vicarage. We need to find out what variety of cat they are. Any volunteers?"

Imogen offered. "I'll ring and ask the vicar in the morning."

"It can't be official. Make something up, and make it sound casual," Calladine suggested.

Ruth offered to find out which hairdresser Elsa went to. "You never know, someone might have been watching her. But for now, I'm going to have to call it a day. Sorry, folks, but I've got to go."

Calladine nodded. "Rocco, the laptops, Elsa's and Megan's. Get onto the Duggan and push them for results. We badly need a lead on this Aiden bloke."

Ruth put on her coat. "Have you considered that this Aiden might be Jason Kent? Just an idea. But it does look like Kent is the one taking the girls off the streets. He wears a disguise. That might be because they know him."

"Good thinking. That makes us getting a lead on him all the more important."

Ruth had just gone through the office door when the phone rang. It was the desk downstairs.

"We've got a Mrs Hayes here, Inspector. She says her daughter, Rachel, hasn't come home from school."

Calladine's stomach turned over. "Show her into the soft interview room, get her some tea, and I'll be down right away."

Imogen was shaking her head. "Not another one? He's not wasting any time, is he?"

"We'd better go and talk to her, and I'm not looking forward to that one bit. Before you join us, would you check with the school? See if Rachel attended today. If she did, find out what time she left."

CHAPTER 16

The look on her face said it all. She was pacing the floor of the room, tea untouched on the table. Rachel's mother was expecting the worst.

She looked at Calladine, tears running down her face. "Rachel is usually home by four. If she's going to be late, she rings me. Today — nothing. I'm worried sick. Do you think he's got her? It's making me ill. If anything happens to Rachel, I don't know what I'll do."

"We mustn't jump to conclusions, Mrs Hayes. Rachel could have gone to visit a friend, a boy perhaps."

"She wouldn't waste her time with boys. She spends all her time with those friends of hers. Well, she used to. Before they got killed." Rachel's mother burst into tears.

Calladine patted her awkwardly on the shoulder. "We don't know what has happened to Megan yet."

She pulled away. "You haven't got a clue what's going on, have you? My Rachel will end up dead too if you don't do something!"

Calladine was about to offer more words and reassurances when Imogen joined them from the incident room. She shook her head. "Rachel wasn't in school today, guv. Were you aware of that, Mrs Hayes?"

When she heard this, Mrs Hayes sank into a chair and sobbed her heart out. "No! She left this morning just like she always did. There was nothing wrong. Rachel was fine. Said she was meeting Sophie on the High Street."

"Imogen, contact Sophie Griggs right away and find out what happened."

Calladine turned to the woman. "Mrs Hayes, do you have any idea who Rachel talks to online?"

She shook her head.

"We believe it's a man called Aiden. Has she spoken about him to you?"

She seemed genuinely surprised. "It's a man she talks to? She told me it was one of those chat rooms for school kids. She was speaking to other students like her. She spent ages up in her room. I'd have stopped her if I'd known. Those children don't understand the dangers. I saw a programme about it on the telly. There are some bad buggers out there."

Imogen returned. "Sophie waited but Rachel never showed up. They'd arranged to meet in a café on the High Street, called 'The Steaming Cuppa.' Sophie says she rang Rachel's mobile but got no reply. She texted too. That was at eight fifteen."

"What route does Rachel take of a morning, Mrs Hayes?"

"Through the estate, down Circle Road, then through the ginnel onto the High Street."

"Ginnel? Do you mean the alley, Byron's Lane?"

"Yes."

"Imogen, get forensics back out there. Get uniform to tape the area off again. Then arrange for a car to take Mrs Hayes home and a FLO to sit with her until we have more news." Calladine turned to the woman. "Rest assured, Mrs Hayes, we will do everything we can to get Rachel back for you."

Rachel's mother didn't look at all convinced. "He's taken her, hasn't he? I'm never going to see my Rachel again!"

* * *

Alan Reynolds lived off the Huddersfield Road in one of a row of terraced cottages that had originally been built for mill workers. The cotton mill had long since shut down and nothing remained of it but a skeletal hulk on the skyline. The cottages had been refurbished and sold on.

The problem was getting up there. Calladine left the main road and took a narrow lane that led up the hill. Halfway along, the road opened up into a parking area and you had to walk the rest of the way, all uphill. He wasn't surprised Reynolds didn't make it into town much. His legs probably weren't up to it.

It was dark by the time Calladine reached the houses. Fortunately most of them had outside lights so he was able to pick his way along the uneven flagstones. Reynolds lived at the far end. Calladine could hear the TV blaring from where he stood. At least Reynolds hadn't gone to bed.

Alan Reynolds greeted him with a broad smile. "Sergeant! It's been a long time, lad. Come in. What brings you up here?"

Calladine smiled back. "Actually it's 'Inspector' these days, Alan. I thought we might have a chat."

Reynolds looked older than his seventy-two years. His face was heavily lined, and he walked with the aid of a stick. He looked as if he carried all the worries of the world on his shoulders.

"I read in the paper about the girl, and about Donnelly being out. I thought I might see you. Bad business. Have you got him locked up?" He showed Calladine to a chair by an open fire.

"No. Not enough evidence to make anything stick."

Reynolds shook his head. "He's a tricky bugger that one. Don't let him wriggle off the hook."

"Things are a bit different this time. The MO, for example. It's not quite the same. To be honest, Alan, we're struggling. And I've been warned off by the ACC. If I go near Donnelly again, well . . . they could have my job."

"The ACC — that would be Kennet?"

Calladine nodded. "I don't remember much about him. What was he like to work for?"

Reynolds waved his hand from side to side. "Tricky. You had to watch your back."

Calladine noticed a photo of Kate on the mantelpiece. He decided to broach the subject cautiously. "Is your daughter not here?"

"No, she's working away for a few days. Kate comes and goes. I don't trouble her. That job of hers takes her all over the place."

Alan Reynolds had spoken about his daughter easily enough. There was no fear in his face, and he wasn't guarded. He mustn't have been contacted. So he didn't know.

"Does she ring you? You're a bit out of the way up here."

Reynolds put another log on the fire. "She left me a voice-mail a couple of days ago." He reached over to a small table, picked up his mobile, and handed it to Calladine. "She's off somewhere in Wales. She says the reception will be bad, and not to worry. Why so interested in Kate, anyway?"

He didn't know, should Calladine tell him? "I'm seeing Shelley Mortimer, Kate's boss. She wondered if I knew Kate, her living in Leesdon. When Shez told me her name I put two and two together and realised she must be your daughter."

"She's a good girl. She does her best by me."

Calladine listened to the message. The young woman sounded okay. "That is her voice?"

Reynolds nodded. "She reckons she'll be back after the weekend. Why do you want to know, Tom? This is more than just casual interest, isn't it?"

Calladine sighed. "We think Kate's been kidnapped, Alan."

His face paled. "Kidnapped! Are you sure? Who'd want to take Kate? Have they asked for money? Because if they do, I've got nowt to give them."

"They are leaning on Shelley. We are working on it. Have you tried ringing her back?"

"Her phone's switched off." He wiped a tear from his cheek. "What are you doing to find her? Have you spoken to her friends? Don't let anything happen to my girl, Tom. She's all I've got."

"We're giving it everything," Calladine assured him. "We expect the kidnapper to contact Shelley anytime. When he does, we'll be on it. The team are good. I'll make sure they keep you up to speed."

Reynolds changed the subject. "That bastard, Donnelly. Why can't you nail him?"

"We're trying. Just when we think we've got him, the evidence turns out to be false."

Reynolds nodded. "Just like the last time."

It was a few seconds before Calladine took in the implications of this. "What do you mean, Alan? I don't recall any false evidence. Everything we got was straightforward."

"I meant nothing, lad. Don't go worrying about all that stuff now. It's history."

"But I do worry. I've got members of my team who think Donnelly didn't kill Annabelle Roper. They're beginning to think we got it wrong, and that he was fitted up." Alan Reynolds didn't reply. "We didn't get it wrong, did we? Tell me we got the right man, Alan."

Reynolds struggled to his feet and shuffled through to the kitchen. "I'll put the kettle on."

"I'd rather you sat down and spoke to me."

Reynolds turned round and faced Calladine. "Kennet wanted him to go down. He was convinced that Donnelly was as guilty as sin. The problem was proving it. Then suddenly we find one of Donnelly's shoes with Annabelle's blood on it. I never knew how that happened and I didn't ask."

"Are you saying it was planted?"

"No, I'm saying the memory is hazy. Take my advice, son, and keep it that way."

"So was he guilty?"

137

"No doubt about it. He killed that girl. I'd stake my life on it. But without that shoe and the necklace, Donnelly was set to walk. It was driving Kennet insane. He knew the score."

"Can you think of any reason why Kennet would want me to leave Donnelly out of it? To look elsewhere."

"That doesn't surprise me. He's big mates with Livings, the vicar who took Donnelly in. He's afraid Livings will try to get Donnelly's conviction declared unsafe. He's a clever man, and greedy despite his religion. If that conviction goes down the tubes, Donnelly could get a fortune in compensation."

"What would be the grounds?"

"False Evidence. We had a blood-stained shoe. Good job we did. It swung the jury. But Donnelly said he hadn't worn that pair in years. They were found at the back of his wardrobe in a plastic bag."

"He was lying?"

"The shoes were expensive, black leather going-out shoes. Not what you'd wear to do what was done to Annabelle. His wife said the last time he'd worn them was at her sister's wedding a decade or so before. She wasn't protecting him. There was no love lost between them, but she was adamant. So how does that happen?"

"You think Kennet was responsible?"

Reynolds shook his head. "I didn't say that. But something wasn't right. You didn't tamper with the evidence, and neither did I." He fell silent. "Make sure you find my Kate. Keep me posted. I'm up here on my own and I hear nowt. Anything happens, you ring me yourself."

"I will, Alan. We will find her," Calladine said.

* * *

It was late, almost midnight, and he was exhausted. Every muscle in his body ached from sheer physical effort. He stretched, rubbed his lower back. What he needed now was a hot bath. But it had been worth it. Just as he'd anticipated, Megan had been completely satisfying. Her lithe young body was even more exciting than he had imagined. He'd not been kind. He'd used her hard, until he was physically spent. Now she lay at his feet, naked and broken. Her blood was pooled on the floor around her head. Beside the body, a keepsake — a cup containing her tongue. He'd put it in the freezer with Elsa's.

"Leave off, Mog." He gently pushed the cat away from the body. A handful of the animal's long coat came away in his hand. "Moulting again. You're becoming hard work, you are." He stroked the cat affectionately.

Shooing the cat out of the way, he laid Megan flat on her back. He stamped hard several times on her chest with the heel of his boot. There was a sickening crunch as several ribs broke. She didn't move. She was dead. He hated the next bit — the cleaning up. Not that anyone would see the mess. No one came here but him. First he would deal with the body. Once he'd got rid, he'd come back and sluice the place down. It would be a long night.

He donned a clean set of overalls and put on a peaked cap. If he was seen, people would simply think he was a street cleaner.

The dustbin was ready. He had taken it from a backyard at the other end of Leesdon last week. A huge number thirty-four was painted on the side. With some effort he manhandled Megan inside. All he had to do now was return it to its owners. He chuckled. Collection day tomorrow.

CHAPTER 17

Friday

Rachel Hayes had no idea where she was or what had happened. It was as if there were a great big hole in her memory where the day should have been. She had been dragged back to consciousness by the clunk of a door being unlocked, followed by grunting and groaning.

Panic set in. There was someone else in this place with her. Rachel's first instinct was to scream for help, but she could barely raise her head. A weak ray of sunlight was just visible. So it must be early morning. Rachel could recall walking to school. Was that today? Possibly not, it felt like longer. She'd been heading for the High Street to meet Sophie. What had happened after that was a mystery. She had a vague impression that she'd been in another room. But she couldn't be sure. It had smelled bad.

Wherever she was, it had no lighting. Rachel squinted. Metres away, a door stood ajar and a man was dragging a long bundle into the building. Silhouetted against the daylight, the man didn't even look her way. Rachel was bound tightly to a chair and there was no way she could get free. She was groggy. Her head ached so much she thought it would burst. She knew this was a chance to call out but she didn't have the strength. Apart from which, Rachel was scared. If she annoyed him, he might hurt her. The man was struggling with whatever he'd brought inside. He was coughing, panting with the effort of dragging the bundle.

Now there was a different noise. Kids were shouting and laughing outside, then a can was thrown against a wall. Rachel took a breath. This was her chance. The man swore. Giving one last look at the bundle, he left hurriedly, locking the door behind him. At that moment Rachel threw up.

The room was dark again. Rachel realised she must have passed out. She was tired and her body ached. Her wrists had been bound to the chair arms with rope and it was biting into her flesh. She had to escape, otherwise she would end up like Elsa. Rachel sobbed into the gloom. The rope was so tight it hurt. She didn't stand a chance.

Rachel looked towards the door. Light filtered through a gap down one side. Its pale rays fell onto the stone floor, illuminating the bundle. She wondered what it was. Her body convulsed with a shudder. Now that her eyes had become accustomed to the gloom, she saw what looked like a dead body.

There was no way she could stay here with a dead person. Maybe she could shout for help. There had been kids outside, they might still be lurking around. She closed her eyes, and took a deep breath. She managed one loud scream that left her throat raw and burning. She hadn't eaten or drunk anything for ages and her mouth was as dry as a bone.

Then she heard it, an almost inaudible moan. Rachel thought her imagination was playing tricks. Then the bundle moved a little. It rolled slightly to one side. Another moan, louder, followed by a whisper.

"Who's there?"

It was not dead, then, and it was another girl like her.

* * *

"They do have cats at the vicarage, two of them. But they are the short-haired, mouser variety. Both are black and white. I told Julian, and he said the cat we're interested in has longish grey fur."

"No joy there then. Thanks, Imogen." Calladine sighed and looked at Ruth.

"Elsa used the hairdresser on the corner of the High Street and Byron's Lane," Ruth told them. "She had her hair cut two days before she disappeared. The hairdresser doesn't recall anyone showing any particular interest. When she's finished with a client, she sweeps up the hair and puts it all in the bin outside."

"So anyone could help themselves?" "That's about the size of it. The hairdressers shares a backyard with at least four other properties. There is a general bin area and the yard is open to the public."

"How do you access the yard?" Rocco asked.

"The hairdressers is on the High Street. The yard is at the back."

"Is there access from Byron's Lane?"

"No."

"Do we know if forensics has finished there yet?"

Imogen shook her head. "No, guv. But they were there last night. The report isn't through yet."

"That hair bobble, anything on the blood?"

"Not yet. I'll get on to Julian about it."

Calladine nodded. "We still haven't had that chat with Gaby Donnelly. Not that I think it'll add anything useful. But we should be thorough, so would you and Rocco sort that? Ruth and I will go have a look at Byron's Lane. See if we can work out what's happening. Back here at lunchtime, see what we've got."

As they took the stairs, Ruth asked, "Anything on Kate Reynolds?"

"I haven't spoken to Thorpe this morning, but Shez says not. She's worried sick. She's afraid the bastard might have got scared and done Kate in. But he's asked for money, so I think that's unlikely. He'll expect to have to prove that Kate is still alive. It's a waiting game, I'm afraid. I went to see Alan Reynolds last night. He has no idea. He'd had a voice message from Kate to say she was going away for a few days and not to worry."

"Did you tell him?"

"Yes, I had no choice."

"And did you speak to Reynolds about our case?"

Calladine looked grim. "Yes, and I wish I hadn't, to be honest. He more or less said that the evidence we had, the bloodied shoe, was planted. Alan reckons the ACC — the then DCI Kennet — was desperate to get Donnelly banged to rights."

"All these years and he's never said anything?"

"Kennet was a bully. Alan would have got nowhere even if he had spoken up. He convinced himself that it was simply a shortcut to getting the conviction. He never doubted that Donnelly was guilty."

"It's not right though, is it?"

"Apparently the ACC is now worried that Donnelly will try to get the conviction quashed. That'll be why he's making a friend of Livings. He wants to be on top of the game. Kennet wants the whole thing burying, and Donnelly leaving be."

"Livings is shrewd, Tom. It wouldn't surprise me if he wasn't using Kennet. All that chat over golf, I bet a lot of it is about the Annabelle Roper case. Kennet had better watch his tongue. A word too many and Livings will cash in."

The High Street was only a few hundred yards away so they hadn't taken the car. Within minutes they were walking along Byron's Lane.

Ruth cast her eyes up and down the short, narrow street. "There's nothing here."

Calladine turned around and scanned the area. Byron's Lane was short and narrow, ending in a narrow 'ginnel' or alleyway that ran between Park Road and the High Street.

Ruth pointed. "No windows or doors along here. The entrance to the properties are either on the High Street or Park Road."

Calladine corrected her. "There will be doors out the back into the yards, and gates into the ginnel."

"Even so, if the girls were taken from here they must have surfaced on either of the main roads. There is nowhere here."

"So why aren't they on CCTV? Megan was seen entering the lane there." Calladine pointed to it. "Presumably she was walking towards the High Street. The café where she should have met Rachel is a few yards to the right once you reach the end." Calladine paced the distance.

"He must have taken them down one of these narrow ginnels then," Ruth said.

Calladine nodded. "Shall we?" They set off down the left hand one. There was nothing to see but walls and the back yards of the shops. "A bit claustrophobic down here, and it's muddy."

"It's worth checking the properties again, Tom. See if any of the shopkeepers noticed anything."

"Apart from the newsagents and the café, they wouldn't be open at that time of the morning. The back gates would be locked." Calladine rattled one of them. "Get uniform to check that with the shopkeepers. Get them to ask if anyone has been broken into this week."

"They didn't disappear into thin air. He took them somewhere."

"Let's have a look down the other one." Calladine led the way back the way they'd come, across Byron's Lane and into the other alley.

Two properties down, the lane opened up into an unfenced stone-flagged yard. "This is shared by those two properties. The butchers here, and whatever that is." Calladine nodded to the two storey brick wall to the right.

"It's the back of what used to be Adams's bakery. The business closed years ago. It's empty as far as I know. There is a flat above, though. Every so often I see it advertised to let in the newsagent's window."

"Is this the only way in?"

"The shop entrance used to be on the High Street, but it's been boarded up for ages," Ruth told him. Calladine had a good look around the yard. The windows on the ground floor were boarded up. "If there's a flat, how does the tenant get in?"

"You can't get in off the High Street anymore, so it's got to be one of these two doors." There was one main back door and another at the far end of the building. "That one probably leads to a staircase for the upstairs flat." Ruth rattled the doors. Both were locked. "The place doesn't look lived in. The windows are so mucky I can't even tell if there are curtains or not."

"Who owns this?"

"I've no idea. We could ask the estate agents who sold it last time around. I remember seeing the sign. It was up for sale for months."

"Jo's?"

"Yes, it will be."

That was a bit of luck. Jo Brandon was the partner of Calladine's daughter, Zoe. Jo was Leesdon's estate agent and Zoe was a solicitor. Calladine was still looking around. "It strikes me that this path is a very good hiding place. You could stand in here and watch folk pass by all day long. Duck down behind those bins and you wouldn't be seen."

"You think he snatched the girls from here?"

"If he did, and he had a vehicle parked in Byron's Lane, then they could be anywhere. But in the meantime we'll deal with what we've got. This area needs another going over by uniform and forensics. I want this path, those bins but more importantly those two properties, searching. That is if they haven't already done them. I'll give Julian a ring from Jo's. We'll get a cuppa while we're there."

* * *

145

Jo Brandon's estate agents was on the High Street. Zoe Calladine had her office on the first floor. The detectives found the two young women sitting together.

Jo winked. "Looking good, Mr C. The regime's going well I see."

"Trying my best, Jo. How about some tea for your overworked dad?" He smiled at Zoe.

"Where were you last night? You were supposed to come over for something to eat and a catch-up, remember?"

He'd completely forgotten. "Sorry, Zo, I'll come another time."

"Not this month you won't. In a couple of days' time me and Jo are off to the States to visit her folks."

"When did you arrange that?"

Zoe shook her head. "I have told you. But you'll have forgotten that too. Jo's parents are celebrating their ruby wedding anniversary next week. They're having a do, and we're invited. We're going to make a holiday of it, travel around a bit."

Calladine followed her into the kitchen. "When are you back?"

Jo shouted through. "A couple of weeks. I've not seen my folks in a while. I'm looking forward to them meeting Zoe. You'll get the opportunity to meet them at Christmas, Tom. They're coming over. So book the time off, and promise not to let us down."

"Christmas! Please, no. I'm still in summertime mode."

Zoe wagged a finger. "It's only three months, so get planning."

"I've organised uniform and the Duggan. Jo and I have gone through the records but they didn't sell the bakery," Ruth called out.

"Well, we did, briefly, then it fell through. The property needs too much doing to it, so our buyer couldn't get a mortgage. Jack Adams took it off the market. As far as I know, he still owns it," Jo explained.

"Do you know if Adams has let the flat upstairs?"

"Not through us, he hasn't. It's a slum, a death trap. But who knows? You'll have to ask him."

"Thanks, Jo, we'll do that."

Zoe addressed her father with a hint of sarcasm in her voice. "If you get lonely while I'm away, there's always Eve. She is your mother after all. I'm sure she'd be delighted to see you."

That might be so, but Calladine found interaction with Eve Buckley hard going. He'd only known her for a few months. Calladine was the result of an affair between Eve and his father, fifty-one years ago. Eve hadn't been able to cope and had handed the infant over to Frank Calladine. Frank's wife, Freda, had raised him, and Calladine had always believed she was his birth mother. The truth about his origins had been kept from him, and Calladine hadn't found out until after Freda's death.

He cleared his throat. "I'll see how it goes. Thanks for the help, but we'd better get on."

As soon as they were on the footpath outside, Ruth tackled him. "It still doesn't sit well, does it? The Eve thing."

"And it probably never will. I just can't think of her as my mother."

"That's because she's not. Freda was. But that doesn't mean you can't have a half-decent relationship with her."

She was right, of course.

"Back to the nick?" Ruth asked.

"I thought we'd look in on Peachy while we're this way," Calladine said.

"Why? We've already spoken to him. He doesn't have anything to say that's relevant to this case. You keep dredging up old stuff and it's wasting time. We've still got Megan out there — remember her?"

"It might give us a lead. There's bad blood between Donnelly and Peachy. I'm convinced that what happened to Annabelle is linked to the current case."

Ruth was annoyed now. "Craig Donnelly — again! You really have to drop this. We're going round in circles. Every time we drag him in, we have to let him go. My advice? Leave the man alone."

Calladine didn't reply. He didn't want to argue with Ruth.

"A far better use of our time would be to get those shops and that old bakery searched. Neither Megan nor Kate was seen again once they'd entered that lane."

"There could have been a vehicle parked up waiting for them."

"Yes, there could, but before we spend hours on CCTV we should look a little closer to home. Megan's hair bobble was found along one of the alleyways."

"Okay — take your point. But we're here now. A quick word with Peachy and I'll get it organised."

They stood outside the bookies window while Calladine rang Julian and arranged for forensics to take another look at the path and back yard.

"We did give it a once-over, but the yard was flooded as I recall. The water people suspected the drains were blocked. The place smelled to high heaven. It is on our list to return once the problem is resolved," Julian said.

"It's alright today, Julian. We've just come from there."

"Leave it with me."

"You hear that, Ruth?"

She shrugged. "If there is anything to find, let's hope the flood hasn't washed it away. But what we really need to do is take a look inside that building."

* * *

When Imogen and Rocco arrived at the school, Leanne Donnelly was waiting with her daughter in the headmaster's office.

Rocco began. "Thanks for coming. We'd like to speak to Gaby about Elsa and Megan." Gaby rolled her eyes. "We know you've spoken to DI Calladine already, but we'd like to go over a few things. We understand that there was no love lost between you, but you might be able to help us."

Gaby's mother answered. "Nasty pair. I've no time for either of them, or that other one, Rachel. They run wild. Do what they want. No one bothers. Certainly not the teachers here. It's disgraceful what those girls have got away with."

Imogen reminded her, "One of the girls is now dead, Mrs Donnelly. Gaby, did you tell your father about the photo the girls took of you?"

Leanne Donnelly was indignant. "No, she did not! Gaby doesn't have anything to do with the man."

Imogen ignored this. "Gaby? He met you off the bus, didn't he? He spoke to you."

Gaby gave a furtive glance at her mother. "That's right. I told him to get lost, that I wasn't interested. I certainly didn't tell him about the photo. What would be the point?"

"You're barking up the wrong tree. You think he did something to those girls out of revenge, don't you?" Leanne Donnelly laughed. "Most unlikely. My ex-husband is a lot of things — an adulterer, a liar, and on occasions a drug dealer. But he is not a killer, Detective Constable."

Imogen stared at her in disbelief. "He's just done time for exactly that, Mrs Donnelly. He was found guilty of killing a young girl."

"He did the time, but I doubt he did the crime," Mrs Donnelly said.

Imogen was curious. "Why do you say that? I mean, there's no love lost between the two of you."

"Don't misunderstand me. I have no time for the man. He did all those years behind bars, and given his history he probably deserved it. But he didn't kill anybody. That's not why I divorced him."

Imogen shook her head. "You said nothing at the time. What evidence did you have?"

"I told the police what I knew. It wasn't much. Not enough to prove him innocent."

"There was evidence that Craig had done it, plenty of it, and that's why the jury found him guilty."

Leanne Donnelly was an accountant with a large Manchester firm, obviously she wasn't stupid or naive. Imogen wondered why she was so sure her husband was innocent of the murder.

Mrs Donnelly snorted. "The police make mistakes too. And they become obsessed. That inspector was on a mission where Craig was concerned, and so was his boss, that DCI Kennet. Between them they were determined that Craig was going down for the girl's murder, guilty or not. Take the debacle with the shoes for example. The entire case hinged on those, but it was rubbish. I knew he hadn't worn them in years! But no one could prove it."

"The evidence was there. It spoke for itself," Rocco interjected.

"I was in court, Detective Constable. I heard all the so-called evidence. Sure, it sounded compelling. I was called. I told them what I thought. When I was questioned about the shoes that prosecution barrister tore everything I said to shreds. Apart from anything else, Craig had another woman. It had been going on for months. He didn't care about me, or the fact that I was pregnant. I told this Kennet person all about his philandering. I spelt it out for him. Gave him the woman's name, address, everything. She was questioned and she gave Craig an alibi. He even told me himself that he'd been with her at the time of the murder. "

Imogen was incredulous. "So, what are you saying? That he was with this woman at the time when the girl was killed?"

"She wasn't believed. The woman was seen on CCTV shopping in the local supermarket the day Annabelle was murdered. She'd told the police that she and Craig had spent the day on the coast."

"So she lied? The fact is you don't know where Craig was?"

Leanne Donnelly looked at Imogen and shrugged. "She wanted to make the alibi sound better, stupid woman. But Craig could have been with her. For years he protested his innocence, but nobody listened. Then he met Livings and for reasons I have never understood, admitted the crime and expressed remorse." She stared at them. "Stinks, doesn't it?"

Imogen looked at Rocco. Did Calladine know anything of this? "Who was this woman, Mrs Donnelly?

"Her name is Natalie. She's married to a low-life called Liam Peach."

CHAPTER 18

Calladine had just pocketed his phone when Imogen rang to give him the information from Gaby's mother.

"Are you sure Leanne Donnelly wasn't telling you a load of rubbish? That's not the name in the file." If Donnelly was seeing anyone, Calladine had expected it to be Dawn Heywood.

"Why would she, sir? There isn't anything between Donnelly and his ex-wife these days. She wants nothing to do with him. I thought you should know right away, which is why I rang you."

"DCI Kennet, you say?" said Calladine.

"Yes."

"Ruth and I are about to talk to Peach now. After that we'll come back to the station. See if you can find out where Natalie Peach lives these days."

Calladine put the phone back in his pocket and turned to Ruth. "Even Donnelly's wife reckons he didn't kill Annabelle Roper. She told Imogen and Rocco that she wasn't even called to give evidence in court. And that Donnelly was having an affair with Peach's wife, Natalie. Apparently that's where he was when Annabelle was killed. That's a new one on me."

Ruth shook her head. "Reason for all the trouble between them? If it's true. But it is a bit far-fetched. Deliberately keeping witness evidence under wraps! But if there is anything in it, then it strikes me more than ever that someone was determined to put Donnelly away."

"Pat Kennet is the best bet. I was stationed at Oldston in those days. I worked that case with him and DI Reynolds. They were obsessed, the pair of them. And I don't recall Natalie Peach being interviewed, or seeing any statements from her."

"This could turn out to be delicate."

"Too right, Ruth. If Peachy's wife—"

"Ex-wife, sir," Ruth interrupted.

"Point taken. If his ex-wife, confirms the story, it could make Craig Donnelly's conviction unsafe. Lead to all sorts of legal wrangles."

"Plus what you've been told already about the blood on the shoe. If Donnelly didn't kill Annabelle Roper, it adds weight to the fact that he has nothing to do with Elsa or Megan."

Ruth was right. The news had not improved Calladine's mood. For his own peace of mind, he was going to have to find Natalie Peach. If Livings was looking into the handling of the original case, he'd be chasing her too. Calladine could do without the entire sorry business coming crashing down around his ears.

Ruth interrupted his thoughts. "Bookies is open and busy."

There were at least half a dozen blokes hanging around, watching the racing on a huge TV screen. But Liam Peach was nowhere to be seen.

Calladine showed the girl behind the counter his badge. "Where is he?"

She smiled at him. "Upstairs, packing. He's off to Spain on holiday."

Not without a long chat and a generous helping of straight talking he wasn't. Calladine indicated a door that opened onto to a staircase. "Up here?" She nodded.

Upstairs, he banged on the locked door. "Peachy! Open up."

"What now, copper? I'm busy packing," he said, turning the key to let them in.

"Tell me about your wife, Natalie, and her relationship with Donnelly."

"That's history. Years ago that happened. I divorced her. Not because of Craig. Problem was, he wasn't the only one. He had history too. Anything in a skirt."

"Do you know where Natalie is living, Peachy?" asked Ruth.

"Lowermill, with her mother. Cottages on Meltham Road, the one with the huge extension on the front."

"Do you still see her?"

"Not for months. After we divorced, we went our own ways. I send a card at Christmas, and sometimes bump into her in Oldston. Apart from that — nothing."

"She had an affair with Craig Donnelly. You don't dispute that."

Peachy scowled. "Behind my back. Some friend!"

"Is that why you and Donnelly fought?"

"Don't remember."

"Natalie alleges she was with Donnelly when Annabelle was killed. Were you aware of that?"

"She'd already left me. Natalie was really into the man. She'd have said anything to get him off."

"So she could have lied?"

"Too true she could. Good at that, she is."

"When are you leaving?"

"Tomorrow afternoon. Can't wait."

"You're going to have to, Peachy," Calladine said. "We will have more questions so you'll need to stay around."

Liam Peach threw the bundle of clothes he'd been holding on the bed. "Bloody coppers!"

* * *

Rachel Hayes pulled again at the ropes that bound her to the chair. "Are you . . . awake? Can you hear me? Please, please, speak to me." She heard another low moan. It sounded as if the girl was coming round. Had he hurt her, or was it the drugs? Rachel sobbed into the dark. "He'll be back soon. He isn't nice. It won't be . . . pleasant. He doesn't care what he does. He's killed one of my friends, and I don't know what he's done with Megan." She paused, waiting for an answer. "We'll be next. I mean it. We have to get out of here."

"Who are you?" The voice was weak but Rachel heard her, and sighed with relief.

"My name's Rachel. I don't know how long I've been here. You?"

"Kate."

Rachel heard her struggling with the blanket he'd wrapped around her body.

"He's tied my hands behind my back and covered me from head to foot in this thing. I'm trying to get free but I can't see anything."

Rachel tried to encourage her. "There's not much light in here, you have to keep trying. We've got to get out. If he comes back we'll stand no chance."

"Do you know where we are?"

"No. I was on my way to school, but I don't know when that was. I don't remember how he got me in here."

"I remember getting off the train. Then nothing," Kate replied.

"Did you see him? Do you know who took us?"

"No, Rachel. He was a scruffy bloke with a long coat, lots of hair and a beard."

Now Rachel remembered. "I think it's the same man that took me."

"I can't get my hands free! How about you?" Kate cried out.

"I'm tied to a chair, hands and feet. I've been trying for hours but the rope's too tight."

Kate whimpered. "If we can't get free, we've no chance."

"I heard people outside earlier, when he brought you in."

"So we shout for help!" Kate said.

"*He* might be close. If he comes back he'll shut us both up — for good."

"We have to risk it. If it's like you say, and he's killed before, he'll do it anyway."

Rachel was scared, and shaking with cold and hunger. What did she have to lose? She opened her mouth wide and screamed again into the damp, dark space. She screamed until she thought her lungs would burst, and Kate joined in, but any noise Kate made was muffled by the blanket. Eventually Rachel had to stop. She was gasping for breath, her face bathed in sweat. Rachel listened. All she could hear was the incessant mewing of a cat.

* * *

It was gone three in the afternoon. Ruth had hoped to leave early, so she could fix the tea and have Harry bathed and ready for bed before Jake arrived. Calladine didn't have to think about the time. The clock could go round all day and all night, but still he worked.

By now they had left the bookies. "Lowermill," said Calladine. "A word with Natalie before we go any further."

"Shouldn't we check in with the others? See what they've got?"

Calladine shook his head. "If anything had come up they would have rung. Sorry, Ruth. I know the day's getting on, but while there's a chance that Megan Heywood is still alive we have to pull out all the stops."

"Rachel too," Ruth added.

He sighed. "I haven't forgotten about her. Bloody case has my head screwed into a tight ball. We need a break, Ruth. Something we can make stick."

At that moment both their mobiles started to ring. It had to be something important. The way the case was going that could mean only one thing. Calladine and Ruth looked at each other. Both spoke at the same time — "Megan!"

They'd guessed right. As they parked up on Taylor Street, Calladine said, "Bloody bin collections are running late today, otherwise her body would have been found a lot earlier."

Ruth felt sick. She'd met Megan, spoken to her. She was a young girl, one of Jake's students. She didn't deserve this. No one did. Ruth nodded at the gowned and masked woman stood outside number thirty-four. "Doctor Barrington."

The pathologist looked at them. "At first glance all I can say is that it looks the same as last time. Teenage girl, seventeen or eighteen I'd say. She is slim with long blonde hair. Left in the bin, naked, a tie around her neck. Hand and tongue as before — and this." She showed them an evidence bag containing a note. Scrawled across it were the two words — *Dead Meat*.

Calladine exhaled. "The description of the body fits Megan's."

"I'll just make sure." Ruth moved forward. The body had been recovered from the bin and laid out on a stretcher. Ruth motioned to the SOCO, who flicked the sheet back for a moment. It was Megan. Ruth nodded at Calladine.

Calladine sighed again. "Same man then. Anything found with her?"

Natasha Barrington shook her head. "Nothing that helps. Clothes are missing, no jewellery. But I won't know for sure until I get her back to the morgue."

"The householders?"

"Number thirty-four — a retired couple, Mr and Mrs Howell. One of your uniforms took the details. He's over there." Natasha nodded towards a young man drinking water from a bottle. He looked very pale.

"Sorry, sir. PC Nigel Hallam. I threw up, couldn't help it," the constable said, his cheeks reddening.

Calladine nodded. "The couple who live here, where are they?"

"Mrs Howell fainted. She's with the paramedics over there. He's with her. He told me everything he can remember. The bin went missing Wednesday and turned up this morning, left outside at the back ready for the collection. They never noticed it was back, or they'd have looked inside."

"Just as well they didn't. Does he know what happened to the bin? Who took it?"

"No. Apparently it happens a lot. Folk blame kids. Mostly the bins end up in the canal."

"See if there's a relative that can sit with them. I'll come back later for a chat. Give them time to calm down."

Ruth shivered. "I'm not looking forward to telling her mother. Doesn't get any easier, does it?"

Calladine nodded at the gathering crowd. "He's there again, Robert Clarke. Shouldn't he be in school?"

Ruth started to walk towards him, to say hello, but then stopped. "It's weird if you ask me. I don't understand what he's up to. He was there when Elsa was found too. You don't think . . . You know — that thing where killers like to hang around the crime scene? Watch reactions. Be there in the crowd when the police are recovering the body."

"You think it's him?"

It was like a light flashing on. "He knew both girls, Rachel too. He has a beef with all of them. I think he's worth talking to, Tom."

"Come on then." They walked towards Clarke.

Ruth smiled at him. "Not working today?"

Robert Clarke looked startled. "Oh . . . Time off — all the extra hours I've done. What's happened?"

"Don't you know, Robert?" Ruth thought he seemed twitchy. He barely looked at them. His eyes were fastened on what Natasha Barrington was doing. Good job the area was taped off or he'd have been right in there.

"Is it Megan?"

Calladine looked at him. "What makes you ask that?"

"I didn't mean anything by it. But she is missing, isn't she?" Clarke replied hastily.

"Yes, it is Megan. Have you seen Rachel this last couple of days?" Ruth said.

"No, but I know she's missing too." Clarke backed away slightly. "Look, I don't know what you're thinking, but this has nothing to do with me."

Ruth noted that he had no coat on. Wherever he'd come from, it couldn't be far away.

Calladine leaned forward and plucked a couple of hairs from Clarke's dark blue sweater. "Cat?"

Clarke smiled, seeming to relax a little. "Mog, my Persian. He's moulting, hence the state of my clothes."

So there it was, staring them in the face all the time. Clarke had a motive, and the opportunity. Calladine brushed cat hairs from his hands. "We'd like you to come down to the station, Robert. Have a little chat."

They had missed it. All the signs had been there, but Calladine had been too focused on Donnelly to see them. Clarke was bullied by those girls. They'd almost driven him out of his job. Not only that, his colleagues knew all about it. For a grown man that must be mega.

Robert Clarke stood rooted to the spot. "Why, what do you think I've done? This is stupid. Why are you getting heavy all of a sudden?"

"Just a chat, Robert," Calladine said again, and beckoned to PC Hallam.

CHAPTER 19

Calladine told her that he and Rocco would do the interview. "Ruth, it's a big ask but would you go and see Megan's mother?"

Ruth nodded. It was a job she hated, but she knew that the awful news might be better coming from another woman. "I'll speak to Jake too. Clarke was wandering about during school hours. We need to know how many times he's done that."

"Ask Jake to come in. Get him to bring any of Clarke's records that he's got. I'll speak to him. The interview will be official, so you can't do it."

Imogen put the phone down. "Clarke's solicitor has arrived."

"We'll give them some time together before we get started."

Ruth was shuffling papers on her desk. "It lets Donnelly off the hook. I must admit, I was beginning to wonder."

"It's still early days," Calladine warned.

Rocco looked excited. "You need to see this! Clarke's details. His address is an upstairs flat on the High Street. Above the old Adams bakery."

It was all falling into place. Calladine looked at his team. "Where are we up to with the search?"

"I doubt it's even started yet, guv," Imogen said. "Everyone available is on Taylor Street, where Megan's body was found."

"In that case the interview will have to wait. Rocco, you and me will go and have a look."

"You'll need keys," said Ruth.

"I'll check with the custody officer. Clarke should have his door key with him."

Ruth shook her head. "We have no warrant in place."

"I believe Rachel Hayes and Kate Reynolds to be in mortal danger. It won't wait."

* * *

Dawn Heywood was distraught. A neighbour was with her when Ruth, a uniform and the family liaison officer arrived. "She's dead? My girl? What about the bastard who did it? You had him and you let him go! If you'd done your job right, this wouldn't have happened." She looked at Ruth with hatred. "She was all I had. My Megan was my whole world."

Ruth explained. "We are interviewing someone, Dawn. Someone different."

"But you can't be sure, can you? You're useless! You dragged your heels and now my Megan's dead. I hope you rot in hell, the whole bloody lot of you!" Dawn Heywood fell back onto the sofa with tears pouring down her cheeks.

Ruth looked at the FLO. If this was hard, the next bit was even worse. Ruth's voice was hardly audible. "Dawn, we'd like you to identify the body."

Dawn screamed at her. "You want me to look at my dead girl? See the things that animal has done to her? Got kids, have you? Could you do it? How would you feel if it was one of yours?"

Ruth's throat felt tight. She couldn't answer.

Dawn Heywood scrambled to her feet. "Get out! And you can take him with you!" She gestured at the uniform.

"Until you can tell me that you have the bastard, and he's going down, I don't want to see you again!"

"Is there anyone else who could identify—"

"I said get out!"

The neighbour spoke quietly. "I'll do it. I've known Megan since she was an infant. I'm practically family anyway."

Ruth nodded. "The officer here will drive you. My colleague will stay with Mrs Heywood. She'll keep you up to date with everything that happens."

Ruth left the Heywood house.

"Heard all the shouting. She's not happy."

Ruth replied without thinking. "What do you expect?" The bloke was press, and she didn't know if news of Megan's death had been officially released yet.

"It's true then? The girl's dead. Still, you got him." He smiled.

Ruth shot him a look. He was fishing. Without another word she made for her car. She drove round the corner and parked up by the common. There she took her mobile from her pocket and rang Jake.

"Have you picked Harry up yet?"

"No, I thought you were doing it. I'm stuck at home with a pile of marking. Clarke's gone walkabout again."

"No, he hasn't. He's in custody. We found Megan. It was awful, Jake." Ruth was sobbing now, she couldn't hold it back any longer. "She'd been murdered, like Elsa. I've just had to tell her mother, and she blames me. She thinks we could have stopped it, and she could be right. We spent too much time looking in the wrong place."

"You've got Robert for the killings?"

"Yes, he's well and truly in the frame. It all fits."

"You're joking!"

Ruth knew Jake would not want to believe this. He'd been on the interview panel that had taken Robert Clarke on, and he'd worked closely with him ever since.

"Calladine wants to speak to you too. He wants to know exactly when Clarke has been absent."

"Does it have to be right now?"

"He will be interviewing Clarke within the hour. He could do with knowing the details of Clarke's attendance in case he needs them."

"I'll get the registers from school. Will you get Harry?"

"Yes. I can't face going back to the nick right now. Dawn Heywood has got me really upset."

"I'll ring Tom. Where is he?"

"I'd leave it for a while. He's gone off with Rocco to search Clarke's home. It could be where he's imprisoned Rachel Hayes and another girl."

* * *

Rocco put the key in the rusty lock. He had to twist and push before the door finally gave. It had swollen with the flood water. It finally juddered open, scraping along the stone floor.

Rocco shivered. "God, it's cold in here."

"And dark. Not a lot of light even with the door open."

The pair stumbled forward, Calladine cursing because he hadn't brought a torch. The ceiling was low and the walls were black with the accumulated grime of years. A few yards further in, he almost tripped over the sleeping form of Kate Reynolds.

"Rocco! Here!" he shouted. The young woman was breathing, and she stirred slightly at the sound of his voice. Calladine heaved a sigh of relief.

"Here's the other one!" Rocco had found Rachel.

"Is she . . . ?"

"She's breathing, but very cold."

Kate was more fortunate. The blanket that had bound her had at least kept her warm. "Ring an ambulance," Calladine told Rocco, as he gently woke Kate Reynolds. She started to whimper. "You're okay, I'm police. You're safe now."

163

He looked over to Rocco. The DC had removed his jacket and placed it over Rachel.

"I can't wake her, guv."

"Stay with Kate and I'll see if I can free her." Calladine's eyes were now accustomed to the gloom. A bench positioned against a wall was cluttered, mostly with old baking utensils. But a section of it had been cleared. Calladine saw a length of rope and several rolls of tape, plus a petrol can. There was also a knife, a vicious-looking weapon. Calladine took it and approached the girl. She didn't stir. He was praying they weren't too late. Gingerly, he cut into the rope that bound her hands, slowly freeing them. The rope had been pulled so tight it had cut into her flesh. Dried blood was encrusted round her wrists and ankles. Gently lifting her into his arms, Calladine carried Rachel Hayes out into the fresh air.

CHAPTER 20

"You didn't like those girls much, did you, Robert?"

Clarke looked puzzled. "Elsa and Megan? They were challenging — teenagers from difficult homes. I don't have the experience, that's all."

"They treated you pretty badly. You lost it on a couple of occasions."

"That's a lie! I did not lose it, that's wrong. I asked Jake Ireson for advice, nothing more."

"Elsa, Megan and Rachel, a nasty trio of bullies who targeted you. I can understand why you'd be upset. I know I would be. It's your first job. You had high hopes, but you got landed with that lot. And you didn't like it, not one bit." Clarke looked uncomfortable. Calladine paused. He seemed to be hitting the right buttons. "That's more or less how it was, eh, Robert?"

"No it was not. Those girls were difficult, but they would have settled down in time. It was because I was new."

"But you couldn't wait. 'Settling down,' as you put it, was taking too long. You were desperate. You had to make it stop. So you killed them both. That's what happened, isn't it, Robert?"

165

"That's a load of bollocks!" Clarke looked at his solicitor. "Can he say those things to me? He's making out that I killed those girls. I didn't. I couldn't!" Robert Clarke began to weep.

"This has come as a huge shock to my client. He needs a break, Inspector. Might I suggest half an hour?"

Calladine nodded, and he and Rocco left the room. As soon as they were out in the corridor, he was on the phone to the Duggan. Calladine got straight to the point. "Anything interesting in the bakery?"

Doctor Roxy Atkins, a senior forensic scientist, was on the line. "Lots, and we're going through it now. Pertinent to your interview with the suspect is an overcoat, a wig and a false beard we found hanging behind the door. Julian is dealing with that."

The disguise. That must mean that Clarke was Jason Kent! "Any forensics he gets from that little lot, let us know straight away." "It'll take time, Inspector. The science we can do, but miracles . . ."

"Anything else important?"

"I'll send you a report when we've logged everything. There was a cat there, a hairy Persian thing. Uniform have handed it over to the sanctuary in Lowermill. We have Clarke's laptop from the flat upstairs too."

"Thanks, Roxy."

Calladine was jubilant. "The 'Jason Kent' disguise was in the bakery. All we need is a forensic link to Clarke and we've got him."

Calladine walked into the incident room. "Guv, Jake's downstairs for you," Imogen told him.

"He'll have Clarke's work record. I'll go and have a word."

Calladine took Jake into an empty office off the main waiting area in reception.

"You can't really think that Robert did this?"

Calladine nodded. "It's looking like it."

Jake rubbed his forehead. "I can't take it in. He seems such a good guy. Keen, ambitious and, apart from this little blip. He'd have done okay in time. Teaching is a hard profession. We're lucky to get the recruits we do."

"You weren't that lucky getting him, Jake. He couldn't handle the kids, remember? He got grief, and he found his own way of giving it right back."

"Getting grief from the kids is par for the course for most newbies in this profession. The kids would have got bored eventually. Apart from Elsa and Megan, who were hard-core troublemakers, the others were fine with him."

Calladine had started to flick through the printouts Jake had brought. "Clarke was absent all day when Megan went missing."

"And Elsa?"

"It looks like she and Rachel were taken early morning. That wouldn't have given him any problems, given where he lives. What did he do for lunch?"

"More often than not he went home. The cat needed feeding, so he said."

"See what I mean? You can't vouch for his whereabouts, Jake, even though he does have a full-time post with you."

"Even so, it's a big leap from nipping home to feed the cat to doing those dreadful things to teenage girls."

But despite Jake's doubts, Calladine was sure they'd got their man.

* * *

"Hi, Ruth! Sorry to bother you at home but I've got some information."

"It's okay. I'm not up to much."

Imogen paused. "Anything wrong? You sound a bit down."

"I've been better. It was awful telling Dawn Heywood. Don't know what I expected, Megan was her only child. But the look of absolute devastation on her face hit me hard. Made me think, what if that was me?" Ruth's voice was shaky.

"We've had a note sent up from uniform. PC Nigel Hallam — he's the latest bright young thing tipped for stardom." Imogen giggled, but got no response. Ruth was really down. "He took part in the search of Donnelly's cottage.

Nothing was found that helps, well that's what we thought. But as they were leaving, Nigel got talking to Livings. The vicar has a display of porcelain figures in a cabinet in his hallway. Nigel said he liked them and the vicar invited him to come and look. Showed him more in the sitting room. Nigel says that he spotted a router in there. He says it was in a glass cupboard along with the Digi-box for the TV. Given that Livings said he had no computer, I thought this was odd."

"There'll be an explanation. But if you're concerned, tell Calladine and he'll sort it."

"Are you not coming back in?"

"I can't face it, Imogen. I'll give it a rest until tomorrow."

Imogen checked the time. It was gone five. Everyone was busy. All she was doing was checking Donnelly's diary against the times Jason Kent was spotted. It was a wasted exercise now they'd got Clarke. She'd go home, but on the way she'd call in at the vicarage herself, and see what Livings had to say about that router. Grabbing the note and her things, Imogen left the office.

* * *

"That stuff in the bakery under your flat. What do you use it for?"

"What stuff? I've never looked. The place is filthy. I don't go near. I use the flat door so I don't have to pass through the bakery to get to my place." Clarke shuddered.

"Never been tempted to explore?"

"None of my business. What stuff are you talking about?"

"I'm talking knives, the rope and tape, not forgetting the petrol. We've got a forensic team going over it with a fine-tooth comb. They will find that the things we found belong to you. That evidence will convict you, Robert. It will be far better further down the line if you tell me the whole story now."

"I didn't do it! How many times do I have to say that? I'm innocent." Clarke's face was inflamed with rage. "You're right,

I didn't like Elsa or Megan. There were times when I could have cheerfully throttled the pair of them. But I wouldn't. I couldn't. I didn't do them any harm!"

"Tell me about Jason Kent."

Clarke looked puzzled. "Who?"

"The alias you adopted to get information from Donnelly. Come on! You visited Craig Donnelly in prison, wearing a disguise. Why was that?" Calladine's tone was even, almost matter of fact.

"What disguise? And I've no idea who Craig Donnelly is either."

"He's the man you visited in Strangeways. You used an assumed name and you consulted him about the murder he committed. You wanted to know what he'd done to Annabelle Roper. You asked for details. You wanted to copy him. We have found the disguise you used in the cellar."

"I don't know how we got to this point, but it's a bloody nightmare. You're talking about people I've never even heard of!"

"Why did you take Kate Reynolds?"

Clarke's eyes narrowed at the mention of that name. Calladine couldn't tell what it meant. "Why choose her? She isn't one of your lippy schoolgirls. She's your age at least. Did you take her for the money? You've asked for a small fortune for her safe return."

Clarke shook his head.

"Kate will speak to us. So will Rachel. They have both been found and are receiving treatment. They will remember what happened to them and they will drop you right in it."

Clarke looked at his solicitor. "Is there nothing you can do? I have no idea who or what he is talking about."

"Come on, Robert, you can do better than that. We know about the disguise. We know you met with Donnelly. And you took the girls after stalking them online. Tell me, how are your computer skills?"

Clarke shook his head. "I've had enough. I know nothing about any of this."

Calladine checked the clock. It was getting late. "We're going to keep you here overnight, Robert. Use the time wisely. You might want to reconsider what you've told us. We'll resume the interview in the morning."

* * *

Calladine and Rocco were on their way back to the incident room. "He's not giving much away, is he, guv?"

"Doesn't matter, Rocco. The Duggan and the two girls will nail him. If I hadn't been so blinded by bloody Donnelly, I'd have seen it before." Calladine threw the file onto Ruth's desk.

"It wasn't obvious. He hasn't left a trail."

"He knew those girls and he didn't like them. The nature of the injuries has meaning. Hands that can't text, or post online. Mouths that can't spout cruel words anymore. It was all there. Ruth tried to tell me, but I wouldn't listen. Where is she, by the way?"

Rocco looked at his watch. "Gone home. Imogen too by the looks of it."

"Not a bad idea. We could all do with a night to chill. We'll pick this up tomorrow. Do we know how the girls are doing?"

Rocco picked up a note that Joyce had left him. "The hospital rang. They're keeping them both in overnight. Kate should be okay to go home tomorrow but Rachel has hypothermia. Her mother's with her and the doctors are sure she'll be fine."

Calladine smiled. "Good result."

CHAPTER 21

Shelley Mortimer grabbed Calladine by his jacket collar, pulled him closer and kissed him. "You are my hero! Thank you for getting Kate back. I thought she was gone for good."

"Have you seen her?"

"Yes, I took her dad to the hospital. He was over the moon that you'd found her. Thinks you're great! Couldn't stop going on about you. Kate didn't say much. She asked about the other girl and dropped off to sleep once I told her the lass was fine."

"I'll speak to them both tomorrow. I'm hoping that between them they can remember something."

"As a reward for doing good, I've cooked tea. Your favourite, steak and kidney pie with chips, and I've walked Sam."

"Where is he?"

"Asleep on your bed. I think I overdid it. Took him up over pots and pans."

"He's getting old. It'll be the hills that got to him."

Shez called back from Calladine's kitchen. "You had a visitor by the way. Your mother."

Calladine could have done without that. All he wanted tonight was to eat and relax. "Urgent, is it?"

171

"Don't think so. Something about a picnic tomorrow, in the park."

Tomorrow was Saturday, so it would be the proms thing. A picnic with his mother along with that side of his family, listening to brass band music. He didn't think so.

"I'll ring her later, or even in the morning. To be honest, I'm whacked."

Shez kissed him again. "Not too whacked I hope, Inspector. I've got the night planned. And don't worry, we're not going out."

* * *

DC Imogen Goode had been banging on the vicarage door for several minutes to no avail. She turned to leave. Livings must be out. It'd have to wait until tomorrow.

"Want something, blondie?"

It was Craig Donnelly. A shiver zipped up her spine. She forced a smile. "Is the Reverend Livings in?"

"Why, you're police. What do you want with him?"

Imogen was in two minds whether to speak to Donnelly about the router or not. After all, the thing might not even be in use, or be a remnant from a time when the vicarage did have a computer.

"When your place was searched, one of our officers spotted a router in there." She indicated the vicarage. "Odd, don't you think, when there is no computer? I was just going to ask the vicar about it."

The man unnerved her. He was staring, his face giving nothing away. Suddenly he smiled.

"Part of the package. You know, TV box, phone and internet. We just never used the internet bit."

It made sense. So why didn't she believe him? "Could I see?"

Donnelly didn't seem too perturbed by the request. He took a key from his pocket and unlocked the front door. "Be my guest, blondie. It's in there, the sitting room."

Imogen walked down the hallway and turned right into the room. She could see the glass cabinet PC Nigel Hallam had mentioned. She bent down for a closer look. The router was turned on, and plugged into the telephone socket, all green lights blinking away. Imogen turned to Donnelly, who'd followed her in. "This is in use."

"You'll have to speak to the vicar about that, love. I wouldn't know one end of them things from the other. Don't even know how to switch it on."

"I'll leave it for now. But tell the reverend that we'll want to speak to him again. We'll send someone tomorrow."

"Why? Is it important?"

Imogen wasn't sure, but something wasn't right. She gave Donnelly a smile she hoped was reassuring. "I wouldn't think so. It's probably nothing." Imogen suddenly wanted to get out of there. Every instinct was telling her to run. She'd come here expecting to find Livings. If she'd known he was out, she would have left it until the morning and brought backup. Imogen made for the front door. "Thanks. Got to get home."

Outside on the doorstep, she heaved a sigh of relief. That was one scary man. Fishing her mobile from her shoulder bag, she rang Julian. He didn't pick up. No doubt he was working late on all the stuff from the bakery. She left a message on his voicemail. "Hi, *honeybun*, going home now, I'll get tea." She rang off, smiling to herself. The serious scientist hated being called anything but his name.

Imogen had left her car on the drive, a good few yards away from the vicarage. It was dark, and there was no one around. The gaunt Victorian church and the tall gravestones cast weird shadows across her path. This place, Donnelly, they had her really spooked. It had been a mistake to come here on her own. She had her key fob in her hand, ready to press the button. Well, a few more yards and she'd be safe.

It came from nowhere. A sudden crushing blow to the back of her head. Imogen teetered on her feet for a moment.

There was another blow, followed by another. Then the world went black.

* * *

When the call came, Calladine was sound asleep. He checked the clock beside the bed. It was two thirty. "Julian? I'm sure whatever you've got can wait until the morning."

Julian's voice was so strained it hardly sounded like him. "It won't wait. Imogen hasn't come home, and her phone's dead."

"What do you mean, not come home? Has she been out somewhere?"

"No, Tom, home from work. I got a message from her timed at seven thirty. It said she was on her way, but she never arrived. Where did you send her?"

"Nowhere, Julian. I thought she was with you. We're busy questioning Clarke at the moment. The part of the investigation Imogen was working on harked back to when Donnelly was in the frame. I thought she'd left work early."

"I'm worried. More than worried. Something has happened to her."

Calladine's heart had begun pumping away. Julian was right. This was way off-beam for Imogen. "I'm going in. I'll check her computer, her messages, see if I can find something."

Shez was awake now, and protesting. "It's the middle of the night."

"Missing DC, one of my own, so it's pull out all the stops time. Sorry, babe. With luck it'll come right, and I'll be back before you know it." He kissed her cheek.

Why didn't he believe that?

CHAPTER 22

As he drove in, Calladine rang Rocco. He didn't want to drag Ruth out of bed, she had enough on her plate with Harry. She could catch up with events in the morning. By the time he arrived at the incident room, Rocco and Julian were already waiting for him.

Calladine threw his overcoat over Joyce's chair. "What was she working on?"

Rocco answered. "Checking Donnelly's movements against Kent's. Given we've arrested Clarke, she may have ditched that and moved onto something more relevant."

Julian looked haggard. "You didn't send her out somewhere?"

"No, Julian. No need. It was all going on here. Ruth had gone home, and Rocco and I were with Clarke. When we came out, I thought she'd left."

"Imogen called me at seven thirty, said she was on her way home."

"Did she give you any hint of where she was, or what she was doing?"

"Nothing that helps. I presumed she was leaving from here." Julian slumped in Ruth's chair.

175

"We'll find her." Calladine put a reassuring hand on his shoulder.

Julian looked up at him. "How? We have nothing."

"Not so, we have CCTV all over this town." Calladine looked at Rocco.

"On it, guv." Rocco sat down at his computer.

"How long will that take? The roads are so busy at that time."

"We have to try, Julian. At the moment, it's all we've got."

Julian stood up. "I'll make us some coffee."

"Good idea. Make mine strong, Julian, and no milk."

* * *

A couple of hours later, Rocco had tracked Imogen's car as far as Circle Road. "Three of the cameras on the High Street were out from six last night for maintenance. I've had a look at all the roads that lead away from the nick. But here she is at five past seven."

Calladine shook his head. "Where was she going? That is in the opposite direction from where you live, Julian."

Rocco was still gazing at the screen. "She must have driven round by the common because after that, I lose her."

"It has to be something connected to the case. She's not going to the supermarket, wrong direction. Neither has she turned off for the Hobfield," Calladine said.

"St James's church is that way."

Rocco was right. "In that case, that's where we'll start."

"I'm coming with you, Tom." Julian put down his cup.

"It's five in the morning," Calladine said, checking the time.

"I don't care. If Imogen went there and she has not returned, the place should be searched."

Calladine doubted he could organise that. They had no evidence. All they'd done was trace her movements and apply a little logic. "We three will go and take a look. But we will have to be careful. We could be entirely wrong. Imogen may have gone somewhere else."

Suddenly the office phone rang, startling them all, given the time. It was the duty sergeant downstairs on the desk. "We have had a report in of a burnt-out car, sir. It was found the other side of the common by a couple of PCSOs. I thought you should know straight away, as the car is registered to DC Imogen Goode."

"Any sign of her?"

"No, sir, the car was empty."

Calladine looked at the others. "Her car's been found — burnt out. It was empty," he added quickly.

Julian was already on his mobile to the Duggan. "Early as it is, I'll get a team down there right away. There could still be some forensic evidence at the site."

"Julian, why don't you go with your team and Rocco and I will go to the church. If we find anything, you'll be the first to know."

* * *

Rocco and Calladine sped towards St James's in the car.

"What do you think, guv?" Rocco asked.

"Imogen knows the ropes, the dangers of the job. I just hope she's not done anything stupid. Got herself into a situation. What I don't understand is why she didn't leave a message," Calladine replied.

"Of course it might be something completely unconnected. Her phone might have died. Her car could have broken down, and kids got hold of it."

Calladine managed a small smile. "How likely is all that, Rocco? But for now, we'll stay hopeful. Until we know the truth, it's all we can do."

The vicarage and Donnelly's cottage were both in darkness. Calladine parked the car outside the main gate. He and Rocco would take a walk around and see if they could spot anything unusual.

Rocco frowned. "Why would she come here in the first place? Donnelly was no longer in the frame. Imogen knew that."

"Perhaps she got some new information. She might have wanted to check something in that diary of his. Any number of things could have brought her here."

A few yards down the main drive, a large patch of shingle had been scraped away. The bare earth looked like a huge scar in an otherwise neat drive.

Calladine squatted down for a closer look. "What happened here, I wonder? This hasn't been caused by a speeding car. It's been deliberately removed. There's a pile of the stuff over there on the grass." He walked across to it. The gravel had been heaped up. Calladine bent down and picked up a handful of it. His stomach lurched. "There is blood on these stones, Rocco." The blood on the top layer had dried, but when he dug deeper, it was still wet, and some got on his hand. This didn't look good. "That's why they've been taken from the drive. Whoever did this probably means to get rid today." Someone had suffered a serious injury here, or had been attacked. So where were they?

Rocco came up beside him, an evidence bag in his hand. Calladine dropped a handful of the gravel into it. "We need that testing immediately." He looked at Rocco. The young man's eyes were wet with tears.

"She's been hurt, hasn't she, guv?"

Calladine patted his shoulder. "We don't know for sure. We don't even know that Imogen came here. Get on to the hospital. See if they had anyone in last night that could be a possible for whoever this blood belongs to. I'll tell Julian, and arrange for the shingle to be taken to the Duggan. You ring for backup. We will make this official. I want a search doing — now!"

* * *

Later that morning, Ruth entered the incident room. "Where is everyone?" she asked Joyce.

"They are all out looking for Imogen. She's missing."

"Missing? How? What's happened?"

"She left here yesterday and never arrived home. Calladine, Rocco and Julian were here in the early hours, working. They got a call about a burnt-out car and left. The inspector is having St James's taken apart."

Ruth shook her head. "I've only been gone one night. Why St James's anyway?"

"I'm not sure, but that's where they are."

"And Robert Clarke?"

Joyce shrugged. "No one has said anything about him."

Ruth fished her mobile from her bag and rang Calladine. "Have you found her?"

"No, and with every passing hour it's looking bleaker. I'm still at the vicarage. Livings is doing his nut. We found blood on the shingle that covers the drive, a lot of blood, Ruth. Until someone explains that, I'm not leaving. We've checked the hospital and they've had no one in from here with injuries."

Ruth closed her eyes and groaned. She remembered Imogen's phone call from yesterday. She'd not been in the mood for listening after the Dawn Heywood incident. Everything the DC had told her had gone out of her mind. But now it was back.

"Imogen got a note from that young PC Hallam," she told Calladine. "He saw a router at the vicarage. I can only think that she went round there to ask about it. I wasn't much help. I was fed up by then. I told her to tell you."

"And I was busy with Clarke," Calladine added grimly. "I think you're right. I think Imogen came here and got involved in something she couldn't handle."

"I should have done something. Rung you myself. Insisted she leave it. But I didn't. The way I was feeling, it went in one ear and out the other."

"You weren't to know, Ruth."

"No excuse. She needed advice. She's only a DC for goodness sake. You have to find her, Tom. If you don't, I'll never be able to forgive myself."

Ruth put her head in her hands. This was dreadful. She could have prevented this from happening. "I'll have to go down there. I can't sit here imagining all sorts," she told Joyce.

"I'll tell . . . Who *do* I tell?" Joyce threw her hands in the air. "Birch isn't here and DI Long isn't back off leave yet."

Ruth grabbed her things. "Tell Thorpe for now."

It didn't take long to reach the church. Calladine had the entire area taped off — the church, the grounds including the graveyard, and of course the vicarage and Donnelly's cottage.

She spotted Craig Donnelly tending to a flower-bed. As Ruth watched, she saw him glance furtively at the search team. She wondered what he was afraid of. Her heart was racing. She could have prevented all this by acting on the information from PC Hallam herself. She wanted to cry. Imogen was young, with everything in front of her. If the girl had been injured, Ruth would be devastated. Ruth took a deep breath. She had a job to do. Emotion had to go on the back burner until they'd found Imogen. "Donnelly!" she called out.

He scowled at her. "I've already spoken to your mates. Couldn't tell them anything so you can bugger off!"

"Then you must know that we're looking for a colleague." He said nothing. "You know what that means, Craig. We'll keep digging until we find something. We won't let up. This is one of our own we're looking for, so we'll leave no stone unturned."

"Nowt to say."

Ruth looked around. "You know these grounds. Where would you hide someone?"

"Get lost. I don't know nothing about no missing copper."

"In that case, tell me about the router."

"It isn't mine. I've no idea what it's doing there."

"Okay, Craig, I'll ask Livings. I'm sure he'll want to help." Ruth walked away towards the vicarage. She was stopped by PC Nigel Hallam.

"Has she turned up yet?"

"No. It was you who gave DC Goode the information that sent her here," Ruth said.

The PC's face fell. "I thought your team should know. I didn't think she'd come here on her own."

"I'm sorry — you're right. Imogen told me about the note you sent up. It was up to me to sort it, but I didn't."

"I hope you don't mind but when I discovered there is a router here, I did some research myself."

"Come on then, what else have you got for us?"

His face brightened. This one's keen alright, thought Ruth.

"When he was inside, Donnelly did a computing course. He was good. Even learned how to program. He got plenty of extra tuition too. His cellmate was an expert — he'd made a fortune selling guns on the dark web."

That was interesting. Donnelly had told them he knew nothing about computers. Ruth smiled at the young PC. She was impressed. "Thanks. That is valuable information. We did ask, but were only told about his religious studies. No one told us he studied computing."

"It was only a short course. I'd imagine what he learned from his cellmate was far more valuable."

"How did you discover this, PC er . . . ?" Ruth wasn't sure of his name.

He smiled. "PC Nigel Hallam."

"So who is your informant, Nigel? Because there isn't much in Donnelly's record."

"I have an uncle in the prison service. He did a stint at Strangeways, ma'am."

Ruth smiled. "Please don't call me *ma'am*. Makes me feel so old!"

He flushed. "Sorry. If I'm stepping on toes, please tell me. I didn't think anyone would mind me fishing around. I want to join CID one day."

"I'm sure you'll make an excellent detective, Nigel. Do you want to come with me while I interview Livings?"

* * *

Rocco nudged him. "Phone, guv."

Calladine hadn't heard it. He was dead on his feet. The caller was Julian.

Calladine spoke straight away, "Sorry, we've not found anything yet."

"I thought you should know that no prints belonging to Robert Clarke have been found in the bakery. On the door, and in the corridor leading to the upstairs flat, yes. But nowhere else."

"So he's never been in there? Of course, he could have worn gloves," Calladine said.

"His prints were not on any of the items we removed either."

"So we've got nothing on him?"

Julian went on. "However, we do have other prints, Tom. Those of Craig Donnelly and Liam Peach. Both have records, so their prints are on file. Donnelly's are more extensive, they're all over everything. Peach's are mostly on the door."

That threw Calladine. He was so tired he was struggling to work it out. "So I was right. This is down to Donnelly?"

"Possibly."

"But if that is so, why leave earrings smeared with your own blood for us to find?"

"I can't answer that."

"Anything on the blood on the shingle?"

Julian's voice was flat. "It's still being processed. I will hear within the hour. I'll keep you posted." He rang off.

"Donnelly's prints are all over that cellar, also Peachy's. We'll have to talk to them again," Calladine called over to Rocco.

"Donnelly is working outside in the garden, guv."

"Let's see what he has to say for himself."

But Donnelly wasn't there. The wheelbarrow and tools he'd been using lay abandoned on the grass.

"We have to find him. We'll do a circuit of the place."

Moments later they spotted Donnelly walking towards a small van parked by the side gate. He was carrying a holdall.

Rocco sprinted after him, calling back, "I think he's doing a runner!"

Calladine came up behind him just as Rocco grabbed his arm. "Going somewhere?" Calladine growled.

Donnelly smirked. "Jobs to do. You've seen how packed my diary is."

Calladine shook his head. "The only place you're going now is down to the station."

Donnelly's smile had little humour in it. "I'd be careful. Livings says he'll get me a top notch brief if you drag me in again. So do your worst, copper. You've got nothing on me."

"That's where you're wrong, Craig. We've got a shedload of stuff. Adams bakery mean anything to you?"

The colour drained from Donnelly's face. He began to struggle against Rocco's grip. "No!"

"I think it does, Craig. Your prints are all over it."

"It's a mistake. I'm being set up. You've got it all wrong, just like before!"

"I'm willing to take that risk." Calladine beckoned to a couple of uniforms. "Take him to the station and lock him up until I get there."

Calladine inhaled deeply. Surely Donnelly couldn't get out of it this time. He would have to talk to Livings. The vicarage door was ajar and Calladine heard Ruth's voice. She was arguing with Livings.

"What are you two doing here?" Calladine asked, nodding at Nigel Hallam.

"Same as you. Looking for Imogen," Ruth told him. "She came here last night to check out what PC Hallam had told her."

"Oh? What was that?"

"There is a router here. In that cabinet to be precise."

Livings stepped forward. "I didn't see the young lady. I was taking choir practice at the community centre. I didn't get back here until about nine."

"What was Donnelly doing during that time?" asked Calladine.

183

"I've no idea."

Ruth pointed towards the cabinet. "This router is plugged in and working. You have a computer, and access to the internet."

"No, I've told you. I do not," Livings insisted.

"Donnelly?"

"He says not."

Calladine shook his head. "He tells lies, vicar."

"Do you mind if we look around?" Ruth asked.

Livings shrugged.

PC Hallam knelt down by the cabinet and removed the router. His elbow jogged the Digibox, almost sending it to the floor. He carefully lifted it out. It wasn't connected. "You don't use this?"

"I hardly watch TV," Livings confirmed.

"This comes as part of a package. So why go for it, if all you use is the telephone?"

"I think it was Craig's idea. He organised it when he first came to live here. Said he was going to drag me into the present day." Livings smiled.

PC Hallam looked up. "There must be a computer hidden somewhere, probably a small laptop."

"I'd like a rundown of your daily routine, vicar. Times of the day when you're out of this building and Donnelly has access to that." Calladine nodded at the router.

"Early morning I'm in church for about an hour. Again in the afternoon, and of course, on a Sunday I hardly get a minute."

"That fits," Ruth said.

Calladine shook his head. "The problem is we have to find it. We've searched that cottage twice now and found nothing."

Livings looked at him. "Perhaps because there is nothing to find, Inspector. Despite what you're telling me, I still believe that Craig is a changed man."

"Craig is as guilty as sin. Tell me — Adams's bakery. What does that building have to do with you?" Calladine scoffed.

"Jack Adams is one of my parishioners. He's very old, sick, and currently being nursed in a care home. He was trying to sell the property, but it's in a bad way."

"Have you ever been there?" asked Calladine.

"No. The bakery has been locked up for years. No one goes there. It's unsafe. Leesdon Council will put a compulsory purchase order on it before long. In the meantime, I have custody of the keys."

"You keep the keys here?"

"Yes, of course. They are kept on a hook in the kitchen along with the others."

"Unsafe or not, there is a tenant in the flat upstairs."

"I organised that for Jack. The rent helps with his fees."

"Aren't there rules about the state of a property which you let out? That place must be breaking them all." Ruth was astonished that he would let part of a building he admitted was dangerous.

"The young man was new to the area and couldn't find anywhere else. He was really desperate, and he gave a generous deposit. Why are you so interested in the place, Inspector? I did warn Mr Clarke about the downstairs rooms. I told him not to go near them. It's the floor that's the problem you see. There is a cellar. The beams that hold up the floor above it have rotted away to almost nothing."

"We found two missing girls imprisoned in there. Plus, we believe it's where Elsa Ramsden and Megan Heywood were killed."

"That can't be true. Who would do such a thing?" The vicar appeared to reflect on this for a moment. "I am willing to help, of course, but I must insist that this thing with Craig stops immediately."

Calladine shook his head. "Won't happen, I'm afraid. You see, vicar, his prints are all over that bakery."

CHAPTER 23

"We've searched everywhere. There is no sign of Imogen. Or of any damned laptop," Ruth said despondently.

Calladine rubbed at his face. "There has to be somewhere we've missed."

"You're knackered, Tom. You should try and grab an hour."

"Rocco is the same, but we can't, not yet."

"Donnelly's prints. That means we've got him. He can't pretend someone else set that up."

"We found Liam Peach's too."

"The two of them were working together? Donnelly I can believe, but Peach has never hurt anyone. Drugs and the like, yes. But never violence."

"You're forgetting that he gave Donnelly a proper pasting about the time of the Annabelle killing," Calladine said.

Ruth suddenly remembered. "He's going away today! He told us yesterday. He's going to Spain this afternoon."

"I told him to stay put. Rocco, get round to the bookies, see if he's there. If not, then get on to Manchester Airport. Ask them to hold Liam Peach. I don't care how much fuss he makes, they must not let him go."

Joyce held out the phone. "Julian's on the line, guv."

"It is Imogen's blood, Tom."

For several seconds neither man said a word. Calladine looked at Ruth and shook his head. "It's definite then. She was at the church last night."

"Yes. And she was injured. It's difficult to ascertain how badly from the blood on those stones. That's the one fact that is keeping me going, Tom."

Calladine nodded at the phone. He had no words. Eventually he said, "We have brought Donnelly in. It looks as if Livings is in the clear. He was out until nine. We are still looking for a computer."

"The blood on the hair bobble found in the alley. That was Donnelly's. We retrieved hair from the wig, part of the disguise hung behind the door. It was short, black hair that had been recently dyed. We have extracted DNA from a couple of tissues found in the coat pocket. That will take longer to analyse."

"Good. With your forensic evidence, and what Rachel and Kate can tell us, we should get this case wrapped up very soon."

Julian Batho put the phone down.

"What are we doing about Robert Clarke, Tom?"

"We should talk to him. You'd better come with me this time. I don't think he likes me very much."

* * *

"We are going to release you, Robert. In a few minutes you will be free to go." Calladine watched the man's face light up.

Clarke kept his eyes on Ruth. "This has been a bloody nightmare."

"At the time you looked like a pretty good suspect," Calladine told him.

"You're saying that I look like a killer? You've got some nerve. You need to get your facts right before you drag folk in here."

Ruth interrupted. "You have a cat, Robert. Cat hair played a significant part in this."

"Mog is into everything. She disappears for days, gets in everywhere, but she always comes back. I suspected someone was feeding her, but I'd no idea she was just downstairs."

"Did you never hear anything? Those girls would have made a noise," said Calladine.

"I thought I heard someone crying one night. I put it down to people walking up and down Byron's Lane. The yard outside the bakery has a funny echo."

Ruth looked at him. "Is there anywhere you can stay? That entire building is being gone over by forensics. Apart from that, it's a death trap. I doubt anyone will be allowed to live there again."

"I'm taking a couple of weeks off. I'll go and stay with my sister."

Ruth groaned. That meant Jake would be up to his eyes in it for the foreseeable.

A PC took Robert Clarke out.

Calladine checked his mobile. "They should have got Peach in custody by now. We'll do him next. Give Donnelly time to consider his position."

"He has to know where Imogen is, Tom. How are we going to tackle that one?"

"He'd better tell us, or I'll break his bloody neck."

* * *

Liam Peach sat down in the interview room. "You do realise I've missed my flight? I won't get a refund. It was a last minute deal."

Calladine smiled. "Can't be helped, Peachy. We need a word. This is serious, I'm afraid."

"Look, copper, I don't know what you think you've got but I'm guilty of nowt."

"In that case, can you explain how your fingerprints got inside the old Adams's bakery?" As he spoke, Calladine turned his gaze to Peachy's hair. At his age, he should be going grey. But his hair was a startling jet black.

"I must have been in there at some time. It'll have been years ago."

"Do you dye your hair, Peachy?"

He smiled and ran his fingers through it. "Linda does it at the salon up the road from mine. It's no crime. I just want to look okay, know what I mean?"

Calladine showed him a photo of Jason Kent. "Do you recognise this man?"

"Never seen him before."

"You see, that's another odd thing. The man is wearing a disguise. An oversized coat, a wig and false facial hair. It's good too, it even got past the officers at Strangeways."

Peachy grinned. "Good for him. What's that got to do with me?"

"It's the wig. Forensics found real hair in it. Just one or two strands, but enough. They are yours, Peachy. How do you reckon that could have happened?"

Calladine was taking a risk. Nothing had been proven yet.

"Someone's made a mistake."

"No mistake. We've been very careful. You see, Peachy, a man wearing that disguise lured two young women to their deaths."

Peachy was adamant. "That wasn't me. You can pin that little lot somewhere else."

"We'd like to, but it's your hair on that wig, and they are your prints on the bakery door. And we know that's where the girls were killed."

Peachy's shifty smile faded away, and he began to look worried. He sighed. "Look copper, I didn't want to get involved, but I had no choice. I owed Donnelly. He was always on my back. My Natalie got herself into bother with a dealer a lot of years ago. I'm not talking small-time neither. The bastard would have killed her. Donnelly gave me the money to sort it. After that, she started seeing him. But ever since then he's behaved as if he owns me."

"Is that why you beat him up, because he was seeing Natalie?"

"Not just that. He tried to set me up for the Annabelle Roper killing. He would have succeeded too, if I hadn't had a stroke of luck."

"Tell me about it."

"Donnelly *did* kill Annabelle. He can scream he didn't until the end of his days, but I know he did." Peachy looked down at the floor. "I saw him put her in that bin."

"You never came forward."

"No one would have believed me. My reputation was even worse back then than it is now. But perhaps I should have done. You lot were having a tough time proving anything. Donnelly was going to run, and Natalie was going with him. He was throwing a lot of stuff out. It was her who got those shoes for me. Silly mare knew they were expensive and thought I'd like them. I knew where Donnelly had left Annabelle's body. The rest was easy."

"Hang on, I need to understand this. You knew Donnelly had killed, but you didn't try to stop Natalie running away with him?"

"Stupid slag deserved him."

"She gave you the shoes, and you put Annabelle's blood on them?"

"Yes I did. And then I put them back in the wardrobe. The rest you know, copper."

At least that meant that Kennet hadn't been responsible. Calladine was relieved. "The disguise, tell me about that."

"Donnelly asked me to sort it, then visit him in Strangeways using the name 'Jason Kent.' I thought I'd get busted straight off, but I didn't. It worked."

"Did Donnelly tell you why?"

"No, and I didn't ask."

"Have you worn the disguise since?"

"No."

"But you've worked it out, haven't you, Peachy?"

"I reckon I have. He killed Elsa and Megan. He used the disguise, knowing you'd spot the guy on CCTV. He wanted me to visit him inside so you'd see a nutter asking how to commit murder. You'd be chasing a shadow, a man who didn't exist. Clever really. Had you lot looking in all the wrong places."

Calladine gave a thin smile. "For a while we were thrown."

Peachy hung his head. "I did try to stop him. I knew those girls. They were okay."

"I believe you. You tried to set him up again, didn't you?"

Liam Peach nodded. "I left the earrings and bobble for you to find. I hoped it would be enough for you to make it stick."

"Unfortunately it wasn't. Did you get Elsa's hair from the salon you go to?"

"Yes, that was easy. I got Donnelly's blood when he came into the bookies one day with a bandaged hand. He'd cut himself doing some woodwork for one of the vicar's old folk. I got Alison to dress it again. The old bandage was covered in blood that was still wet."

"You'll give a statement and testify in court?"

Peachy nodded.

"Good. Now, perhaps you can help us with another matter. We believe Donnelly is holding one of our team. We've searched the vicarage and the cottage with no luck. Do you know if Donnelly has another place he uses?"

Peachy shook his head. "Apart from the bakery, there is nowhere."

"There has to be. We know he has a computer, but we can't find that either. Think, Peachy. Has he ever said anything? Hidden anything for you?"

The shifty look was back. "Well, yes, he has, and he's still got it."

"What?"

"If I tell you, I'll be incriminating myself."

Calladine leaned forward. "A woman's life is at risk. Right now I don't give a damn about drugs, guns or anything else you're trading in."

"Not guns, just drugs. Nothing heavy, either. Just enough to make me a bob or two. Get me out of debt."

Calladine was wracking his brain. "We've been all over that place. We didn't find anything. If Donnelly doesn't stash stuff at the bakery, then he has to have somewhere else."

"There isn't anywhere else."

Calladine suspended the interview.

"At least he'll testify. Looks like we've got Donnelly, Tom."

He looked at Ruth. "We still need forensics. Right now, I'm more concerned about Imogen. Donnelly is a known killer. Young, blonde women are his thing."

"Do we interview him next?"

Calladine nodded.

CHAPTER 24

Donnelly sat down. "This is getting tedious."

Calladine came back at him. "For you and us both. We know about the bakery, Craig. We know what you did there. We've found your prints all over items used to imprison and murder two girls."

"Got me banged to rights, then." Donnelly leaned back in the chair and folded his arms.

"What? No argument this time? Not going to shout and bluster about your innocence and how we're picking on you?"

"No point. I'm tired of it all. I won't stop. I can't. The only way to make sure I don't kill again is to lock me away. I tried to tell Livings, to make him see what a mistake he was making taking me on. But he believed in me, you see. He truly thought that a home, a job and the comfort of the church would get me through." He hung his head. "But he was wrong. I can't change." The room was silent. Donnelly looked Calladine in the eyes. "You know that too, don't you?"

"You are admitting it, then? The murder of Elsa Ramsden and Megan Heywood, plus the abduction of Rachel Hayes and Kate Reynolds?"

He grinned, boastful again. "Nice touch that, don't you think? Given it was her dad who put me away the first time. The Reynolds girl was going to get me a fortune. I'd have had the money to scarper."

"Do you have a computer, Craig?" Ruth asked.

"A laptop. Easier to hide."

"So you groomed those girls online, posing as a young lad called Aiden," Calladine said.

"Easy-peasy. Stupid tarts lapped it up. You have no idea how simple it was. Chat them up, lure them in, and bingo! It was all part of the game. But after a while the game gets boring."

"Why those girls in particular, Craig?" asked Calladine.

"Why not? I was going to kill anyway. They were easy targets."

"Were you concerned that they had upset your daughter?"

"I thought about it. Upsetting my Gaby was not a good idea. But if it hadn't been them, it would have been someone else." He gave Calladine a chilling smile. "I'm a killer, Inspector. It was my intention to come back to Leesdon and make a name for myself." He paused. "I think I've done that alright, don't you? Maybe one of them psychobabble people will tell me why one day. But the simple truth is, I get off on it."

Listening to this was sickening.

"Putting things right for Gaby was a bonus. There'll be no more nasty texts, harsh words or pictures texted around. I've made sure of that."

His words sent an icy chill through Calladine. Beside him, Ruth held her breath. Calladine's voice shook slightly as he asked the next question. "What have you done with Imogen Goode?"

"Wouldn't you like to know, copper? She's another young blonde that had the bad luck to come my way." A wide smile accompanied these words, and Donnelly's eyes lit up. He was playing them, and enjoying it. It was the only power he had left. Calladine's stomach turned. This man was not going to help them.

"This is a chance for you to redeem yourself, Craig," Calladine tried. "Help us and perhaps we can help you."

Donnelly laughed. "I'm not an idiot. No one is going to help me, copper. What they are going to do is lock me up and leave me to rot!"

"Where is she?" Calladine roared at him. "Tell us, Craig!"

"Go to hell, copper!"

* * *

"Search the place again?" Ruth sounded hopeless.

Calladine was pacing. This should be a good time. The team had their man. They should be celebrating. Instead they were strung out and worried to death about Imogen.

Ruth had an idea. "Peachy asked Donnelly to hide drugs for him. We haven't found them either. So let's get a dog team on it. If they find the drugs, chances are they'll find Imogen — and that damn computer too."

She was right. Calladine turned towards her and smiled. "Good one, Ruth. I should have thought of that myself."

"You've not slept. Your brain's running on empty. And it's only a good idea if Donnelly's hiding place is in the church grounds."

* * *

The dog team was on site within the hour. Calladine, Rocco and Ruth were watching.

"Anyone told Julian?" Ruth asked.

Rocco answered. "I did. He'll join us shortly."

"You don't think he's buried her, do you, Tom?" asked Ruth.

"No. Donnelly didn't have anything to do with the graves. And there have been no funerals here all month. The graveyard is full."

"Over here!" At least two of the dogs were showing a particular interest in a large grave.

The detectives hurried across. Calladine's heart was in his mouth. He didn't usually have any time for religion, but he was praying now. "Big for a grave."

"That's because it isn't," Ruth told him. "It's a family vault. The Brayshaw family, to be precise. The cotton baron, Elias Brayshaw, was really wealthy. The lot of them must be in there."

"Why didn't we notice this before?"

"The entrance is half buried. There's one big stone, plus that carved angel. It looks like an oversized grave, that's why."

Rocco was pulling some of the weeds from the path. "So what exactly is it?"

"Essentially it's a stone room. It'll contain the coffins of that lot," Ruth nodded at the inscription.

Calladine shouted across to the uniformed officers. "Get it open!"

"There are more of them dotted all over the graveyard," Ruth pointed out.

"The dogs like this one." Calladine felt dreadful. This was one of the worst moments of his life.

"New lock, sir!" a PC shouted back.

"Smash it open!"

* * *

The paramedics brought Imogen's body out of the vault. Ruth buried her face in a hanky and wept.

"Smashed over the head with something flat. A spade looks likely." Natasha Barrington told them. She too had tears in her eyes. Julian was stood to one side, an odd expression on his face. "You'll have to look after him," Natasha told Calladine.

"Would she have known?"

196

"No, the head injuries are extensive, Tom. Imogen would have been dead before she was dragged in there."

Calladine stood beside Ruth. "It is something at least."

"That could be any one of us being carted away in that ambulance, Tom. It's too awful. Imogen was young. Julian won't cope, we won't cope! She was part of us all."

Ruth turned to Calladine and he held her tight. He rubbed a hand through her hair as she sobbed against his chest. He felt the hurt like a physical pain. He was wrung out emotionally and grossly overtired. He felt almost light-headed. Ruth looked up at him, about to ask a question. Before he knew what he was doing, he had kissed her.

Ruth pulled away. "What are you doing? What is this?"

"Sorry, I thought you needed a hug."

"You kissed me!" The words came out in a hiss. She obviously didn't want anyone to hear.

"It was a simple gesture of affection. We're both cut up over Imogen."

"Don't do anything like that again, Tom Calladine!"

She seemed angry but her cheeks were flushed. Calladine left her and went to find Julian. He had no idea why he'd kissed her. But was it so strange? Ruth had been in his life longer than anyone. He'd known his mother for less than a year. His daughter, Zoe, had been unknown to him until she was a grown woman. He'd never analysed his relationship with Ruth. But what he did know was that he didn't want to lose her. He needed her in his life, and not only at work.

Ruth caught him up and grabbed his arm. "I understand. But you scared me. I can cope with the Tom Calladine I work with, but nothing more."

He looked at her and gave a sad smile. "I'm sorry."

"What I'm saying, Tom, is don't ruin what we've got. You are a good friend. I love you as a friend. Let's leave it at that."

"Love me, do you? And I had no idea." He tried to make a joke of it but his words died away. Calladine saw Julian, weeping on his own.

Ruth continued. "Don't push it. We're none of us in a good place right now. We have to keep it together for the others. You, especially."

"I'll try. Will you help me?"

"Yes, but no more hugging, alright?"

"OK."

THE END

CHARACTER LIST

Detective Inspector Tom Calladine
He is single, just past fifty. He is tall, his hair used to be dark but is now greying and is cut close to his head. He has been on a health kick and lost weight, and improved his fitness. His daughter is called Zoe, she resulted from his short-lived marriage and he only found out about her recently. He has had a chequered love life. Currently the woman in his life is Shelley Mortimer.

Detective Sergeant Ruth Bayliss
She is single in *Dead Wrong* but meets someone — teacher Jake Ireson, in *Dead Silent*. She's in her mid-thirties, likes bird-watching. Works with Calladine at Leesdon police station. She has been on maternity leave but is about to return to work. Her baby son, Harry, is six months old.

Detective Constable Simon Rockliffe — Rocco
A solid team member. He works hard and gets results. He is tipped to go far. He was attacked on the Hobfield in *Dead Wrong*. He has hinted that he might have a girlfriend but is giving nothing away.

Detective Constable Imogen Goode

She is the IT expert of the team. She is intense — very keen on her work — a bit of a nerd. Imogen has long, blonde wavy hair, a buxom figure, and is keen to advance. She is going steady with Julian Batho — the forensics expert. They have recently bought a house together on the same development as Zoe Calladine and her partner live.

Detective Chief Inspector Rhona Birch

Rhona has the reputation of being a 'hatchet queen.' It is rumoured that she hasn't more than two years at any station. Much to Calladine's surprise, it turns out that she has a son and an ex-husband. Calladine sees a new, emotional side to the woman when her son goes missing in Australia.

Detective Inspector Stephen Greco

Detective at nearby Oldston police station. Ambitious.

Doctor Sebastian Hoyle

Pathologist — now retired but working as a locum at Leesdon Health Centre. Often referred to as the doc.

Forensic scientist Batho

Unmarried, but in a long-term relationship with Imogen Goode. He is hardworking and passionate about his work. Not particularly good-looking. He is now working at the Duggan Centre and has been elevated to Professor Batho.

Monika Smith

Care-home manager and former girlfriend of Calladine.

Freda Calladine

Tom's late adopted mother — was resident in the care home run by Monika.

Eve Buckley – nee Walker

Eve is Calladine's biological mother. They met for the first time in *Dead List*. He learned the truth about his birth from a letter his mother left for him to open after her death. Eve wants to try and put things right, to bring Calladine into her family.

Samantha Hurst

Eve's daughter and therefore Calladine's half-sister. She is a doctor at a hospital in Manchester. They met during *Dead List* but though he knew who she was, Samantha had no idea about him.

Shelley Mortimer — known as 'Shez'

Calladine's latest girlfriend. She is ten years his junior. Very attractive with chin-length, black hair. She is rarely seen without make-up, particular her signature red lipstick. Shez runs a model and escort agency on the outskirts of Manchester.

PC Nigel Hallam

Young, curly blonde hair and tipped to go far. He is keen to progress to CID.

DI Alan Reynolds

Now retired. Still lives in Leesdon with his daughter Kate, who works for Shez. He was Calladine's DI when he was a DS.

ACC Pat Kennet

Now the Assistant Chief Commissioner, he was Reynolds' DCI when he was in the force.

THE JOFFE BOOKS STORY

We began in 2014 when Jasper agreed to publish his mum's much-rejected romance novel and it became a bestseller.

Since then we've grown into the largest independent publisher in the UK. We're extremely proud to publish some of the very best writers in the world, including Joy Ellis, Faith Martin, Caro Ramsay, Helen Forrester, Simon Brett and Robert Goddard. Everyone at Joffe Books loves reading and we never forget that it all begins with the magic of an author telling a story.

We are proud to publish talented first-time authors, as well as established writers whose books we love introducing to a new generation of readers.

We won Trade Publisher of the Year at the Independent Publishing Awards in 2023 and Best Publisher Award in 2024 at the People's Book Prize. We have been shortlisted for Independent Publisher of the Year at the British Book Awards for the last five years, and were shortlisted for the Diversity and Inclusivity Award at the 2022 Independent Publishing Awards. In 2023 we were shortlisted for Publisher of the Year at the RNA Industry Awards, and in 2024 we were shortlisted at the CWA Daggers for the Best Crime and Mystery Publisher.

We built this company with your help, and we love to hear from you, so please email us about absolutely anything bookish at feedback@joffebooks.com.

If you want to receive free books every Friday and hear about all our new releases, join our mailing list here: www.joffe-books.com/freebooks.

And when you tell your friends about us, just remember: it's pronounced Joffe as in coffee or toffee!